To be witness to a perfec moment of absolute perfection. Our birth, and perhaps our death. Two seconds of perpetual individualism wrapped in precision, provided by nature. Sweet those moments are. Sweet as honey on one's tongue.

The beekeeper longed for either. To be born again, or to die. His mind now softened by generations, he could no longer draw a line between the two. Instead, he traveled solo through time and space. His memories, tapestries of trial and error. His mournful stare resting on nothing particular anymore. In a moment lost, yet not so long ago, the beekeeper was life itself, in all its pleasure and pain. He was here, of this earth, bonded by temperament, and provoked each morning by the subtle warmth of the sun upon his youthful face.

In this, his past life, he learned in short time that trust was universal. His netting, his hat, his gloves permanent fixtures on a wooden coat rack upon the porch. The subjects and their hum, they softened with time, as did he. Of yellow and black, of contrast to blue and the sky that painted their background, they were slaves to their dance, bearers of the sweetest fruit as they sang their instinctual song. They were a whole in some ways. A lot like him--one single entity. The tribe of stingers and pollen-swollen legs acted as one, a unison with which the human race would never come to terms. It would be our downfall, the beekeeper concluded, a passing thought ripped from the void and slammed back again, a pain in the back of his skull. That was why, no matter how we lived our lives, we died alone and scared in the end.

"It's time," the Beekeeper said and struggled to raise his chin.

A shadow moved across his room and acknowledged him with a sigh. It was enough for him, his strength stolen along with his youth, the bitterness he thought settled long ago. Visions drifted between the soft fragrance of fresh grass and linen. He ran between the white sheets Mother left on the line and magnificent clouds he was certain were born the very day he inhaled that first cusp of mortal air. Substance was life at tender age and false assumption. Such security, and so far from Death's reach was childhood. So sensuous, and how very misleading it was to run with bones still soft and unbreakable.

"I was young," he whispered to the shadow,

All the best
Heidi
2008

"fantastic set of tales... Weirdly gave me everything it promised and more... Top notch writing. I'll be recommending this to anyone and everyone. Stunning!"

~White Russian, Cocktail Reviews

Other books available at Wild Child Publishing:

Bad Things by J.G. Craig
Dark Roads & The Boy in the Grey Tracksuit by J.G. Craig
Decimate by Various Authors
Fade To Pale by James Cheetham
How To Avoid Writer's Hell by Faith Bicknell-Brown
The Immortal Soul by Mack Mani
Impressions by Matthew Babcock
Iron Horse Rider by Adelle Laudan
Odd Pursuits by Robert Castle
Oh, Ragnarok! by Gabriel Llanas
Pervalism by M.E. Ellis
Quits: Book 1: Demons by M.E. Ellis
Quits: Book 2: Devils by M.E. Ellis
Shutterbug by Daniel I. Russell
Soul Haven by Sonja Baines
Weirdly: A Collection of Strange Tales by Various Authors
The Writing on the Wall by James Goodman

Stay up to date with what is happening at WCP:
WCP/FB News Blog: http://wcpfbnews.blogspot.com/
WCP MySpace Page: http://www.myspace.com/wildchildpublishing/

Weirdly: A Collection of Strange Tales

by

C.T. Adams & Cathy Clamp

Faith Bicknell-Brown

James Cheetham

Marva Dasef

M.E Ellis

Bernita Harris

Stacia Helpman

Lion Irons

Rae Lindley

Rosa Orrore

Amanda Tieman

Wild Child Publishing.com
Culver City, California
Weirdly: A Collection of Strange Tales
Copyright © 2007

Weirdly: A Collection of Strange Tales by C.T. Adams & Cathy Clamp, Faith Bicknell-Brown, James Cheetham, Marva Dasef, M.E Ellis, Bernita Harris, Stacia Helpman, Lion Irons, pseudonym, Rae Lindley, Rosa Orrore, pseudonym, Amanda Tieman

Cover illustration by Wild Child Publishing © 2007

For information on the cover art, please contact covervan@aol.com

All rights reserved. No part of this book may be reproduced or transmitted in any form without written permission from the publisher, except by a reviewer who may quote brief passages for review purposes.

This book is a work of fiction and any resemblance to any person, living or dead, any place, events or occurrences, is purely coincidental. The characters and story lines are created from the author's imagination or are used fictitiously.

Editors: M.E Ellis & Faith Bicknell-Brown

ISBN: 978-1-934069-68-4 - ebook
978-1-934069-76-9 - paperback

Wild Child Publishing.com
P.O. Box 4897
Culver City, CA 90231-4897

Printed in The United States of America

Contents

C.T. Adam & Cathy Clamp
Those Who Won't Be Missed — 7

Faith Bicknell-Brown
Little Karen — 15
The Violin's Cry — 21
The 63rd President — 26
Uncle Willy's Cure — 31
Collecting Data — 37

James Cheetham
The Beekeeper — 39

Marva Dasef
The Country Faire — 49
The Hunter — 53
Coward — 55
Heather's Pain — 57

M.E. Ellis
The Game — 62
Serenity Sea — 65
The Stanza — 66
Maurice's Job — 69
A Thousand for One — 72
You Shall Be Heard — 76
Manhunt — 78

Bernita Harris
Stone Child — 81

Stacia Helpman
Anya 100

Lion Irons
Double Omega 113

Rae Lindley
A Day in the Life of Simplicity 125

Rosa Orrore
Know It All 139

Amanda Tieman
The Surprise 146
The Sickness 161

Those Who Won't Be Missed
by
C.T. Adams & Cathy Clamp

The night was clear and cold. Faint crystal stars flickered in the distance. Snow glittered frigid white in the stark moonlight. My breath misted the air, and I huddled deeper into my woolen overcoat. I rummaged with numbing hands in the deep coat pockets for my lighter.

I hate the cold, but I was glad to be outside right now. Better freezing than in *there*. "There" was a nursing home...excuse me, extended care facility. The place where the people of our fine city and the surrounding areas sent the unwanted detritus of humanity to await death. I can stand it for a while, but after an hour or so, the overpowering combination of antiseptic and urine makes me claustrophobic.

I don't fear death. Why should I? I am a priest and a fairly good one. But, I do fear that in-between state—fear hovering between life and death where there is only isolation and suffering. But it is my job to come here to say the rosary with the faithful Mrs. Reilly and Mrs. Romano. I give last rights to those who need it, when the time finally comes that they are released from their mortal bonds.

I had started coming here as a favor to Todd. My best friend since grade school at St. Francis, he had matured into a dedicated doctor who cared passionately about the plight of the infirm and elderly. He struggled to stay on top of the myriad of duties. I could only watch as he drained himself to the dregs in an attempt to better their final days.

He asked. I came. I visit with the Catholics always, but with non-Catholics too. One or two are even coherent enough to recognize me. Poor lonely souls. Shuffled off to die. They're lucky to see their children for visits at Christmas and Mother's day. It's my job to offer them comfort but there's little to be had.

It's easier for the ones whose minds go. Easier not knowing that they've been discarded with the trash.

"Here father." Her words interrupted my musings. A flash of light sprung up in the darkness and a disposable lighter flared in front of my cigarette.

"Thanks." I took a long puff, the smoke curling and joining the mist of our breaths in the winter air.

We didn't speak further, but the silence wasn't uncomfortable. We'd seen each other here often. Sunday afternoons, Wednesday nights. I visited Mrs. Reilly and Mrs. Romano. I wasn't sure who she came to see. Probably a grandmother...maybe a mother, though she seemed a bit young for it.

Those Who Won't be Missed

In her mid-twenties, I'd say, tall and slender, but athletic. In the silver moonlight, her long curls were the color of dried blood, but I'd seen her in better light. A natural redhead, complete with freckles and the greenest eyes I'd ever seen. She had a face you'd remember. Strong features—skin as smooth as marble and about as warm. She reminded me of a statue I'd seen at the Cathedral of an angel, her sword pinning a demon to the ground.

I'd asked Todd about her. She had the look of the Irish and lived close enough to visit often. It was a wonder that I'd never seen her at St. Michael's. Not even on Christmas or Easter. He told me her name—Francis Coughlin, but either didn't know or wouldn't tell me her story. He would only say that she was "from the neighborhood." On impulse, when I got back to the rectory I asked Monsignor Sheehey if he knew of her.

Monsignor, an old man, had been large once but now shriveled with age. His skin sagged loosely on his broad bones. Age spots marred his hands and showed through his thinning hair. I spoke to him as he sat at the kitchen table, his gnarled fingers wrapped around a ceramic coffee mug. "Such a sad thing." He shook his head, and for almost the first time he actually looked his seventy years. "Tragic."

"What happened?"

It wasn't a long story. Nor an uncommon one. But he was right, it *was* tragic. Francie's mother was a beautiful flirt. Her father an abusive drunk. One afternoon, Francie had come home from a school softball game to find her mother dead and her father strangling her younger sister. Francie had smashed his head in with the ball bat. Her sister, Meg, had survived...but it might've been better if she hadn't. She was brain dead.

"But she could confess—" I objected, pulling a cup from the cabinet and filling it with strong black coffee from the pot on the warmer.

"Ah, Patrick." Michael Sheehey sighed and pulled his right hand away from the warmth of the cup long enough to loosen his clerical collar. "A good confession requires repentance. Francie isn't sorry. She did her time in juvenile hall, finished high school at public—" His voice trailed off. He sounded almost as tired as I felt.

"And she visits her sister every Sunday and Wednesday," I concluded.

We finished our coffee in silence.

* * *

In the days that followed, I made a point on my visits to stop in and visit Meg Coughlin. There was a resemblance between the two sisters, but it was the differences that were the most striking. Meg had been bedridden for years. Her pale skin lay flaccid over her bones, with no muscle tone or strength. Her hair, the same red as Francie's, had been cut short to make it easier to care for. Most of all, there was no "life" to her. Meg lay motionless on her hospital bed, the blue cotton gown rising and falling with her steady breathing: alive but not living. Even at rest, Francie vibrated with contained energy. She was so intense it was almost frightening.

I'm sure Francie guessed that I prayed for them both. I suspect the knowledge gave her more amusement than comfort. Still, twice each week we would meet outside the building to share a smoke.

We didn't talk, which was a shame. It was a lonely time for me. The winter weather made Michael Sheehey's bones ache, souring his disposition; and Todd...well, the strain was starting to tell. Circles dark as bruises appeared beneath his eyes, and he was tense, jumpy. Patients were dying.

"Not," I pointed out, "an unusual occurrence in a facility such as this."

"This is different," Todd argued. "It's just *wrong*. Doesn't it strike you odd that none of the fallen have families to raise questions or authorize an autopsy? They're all people who won't be missed."

"What are you saying?" I asked.

"I'm not sure," he admitted, his expression darkening. We didn't speak of it further. One of the orderlies approached. Todd changed the subject abruptly and walked with me as far as Mrs. Romano's door and, in an uncharacteristically sentimental move, gave me a fierce bear hug. "I love you like a brother, Patrick."

I stared, dumbstruck. I loved him too. But never in all of the years we'd known each other had either of us voiced it.

I'm not sure what I would've said, how I would've responded, had Mrs. Romano not called out my name. I spun at her call and, by the time I'd turned back, Todd was gone. He walked at a brisk clip down the hall, the green suited orderly at his side.

I promised myself I would stop by his office on my way out—force him to go to dinner with me, get him to unburden himself. I ran through the decades of the rosary on autopilot, my mind elsewhere. When Mrs. Romano finally fell into an uneasy sleep, I slipped out of the room, my coat slung over my arm.

I was just pulling the door closed behind me when the lights flickered and went dead. The darkness lasted only a moment. Emergency lights flared to life almost immediately. Harsh spotlights mounted on boxes at ceiling height either threw objects into stark relief or cast them into deep shadows. Patients cried out in alarm from their rooms. Nurses and assistants made reassuring noises as they moved in a controlled half-run down the hall

Those Who Won't be Missed

toward the "critical" wing where alarms sounded an ominous cacophony. In the distance, I heard the emergency generator struggling to come to life.

In the midst of the confusion, I accidentally slammed into Francie. She whirled, staring at me with eyes wide and dark with alarm. Her jacket fell to the ground, and I caught a glimpse of a bandaged wrist and small round scabs that were almost hidden beneath the collar of her white cotton blouse. Her reaction surprised me. She had never struck me as the type to panic.

"I'm sure it's nothing," I said, giving her a reassuring smile and forcing down my own growing unease. The generator still hadn't kicked in, and while I'd seen the majority of the staff go by, I saw no sign of Todd.

"My sister is missing."

I stared at her for a long moment, stunned. It made no sense. It was not as though Meg could just wander off. What in the *hell* was going on? And *where* was Todd?

I followed Francie as she made her way down the maze of connecting corridors. I knew that we were heading to the farthest corner of the building—to Todd's office. I clutched my coat to me with sweating palms, shoulders tight with tension I could not explain. My heart thudded so loudly that I was sure Francie could hear it.

Todd's office was around the far corner, its entrance in deepest shadow. A small half-wall kept the emergency light from penetrating. Francie turned abruptly, shoving me hard. I half-fell, and my head slammed against the tiled wall. My legs tangled in the weight of my overcoat.

I steadied myself with one hand, rising slowly. I opened my mouth in accusation but then stopped, tongue suddenly dry with purest terror.

Todd Murray lay sprawled on the tile floor. Two shadowy figures knelt beside him, feeding. I heard wet sucking sounds over the clamor of alarms, my own harsh breathing, and thudding heart.

They turned toward us, hissing, and I caught a glimpse of fangs dripping with Todd's life blood. My mind numbed. I couldn't move—could only watch mesmerized as Meg lurched toward me, green eyes feral.

She approached with jerky, awkward and unpracticed movements. I should have run but my muscles were frozen. I stared helplessly as she stumbled forward, each movement flashing leprously pale skin.

"Meggie?" Francie's harsh tone caused the creature to turn. Only when her eyes left mine did I regain control of my body. I knelt on the floor. My hand instinctively reached for the string of rosary beads that had fallen from my grasp. The cold touch of the metal crucifix cleared the fog from my mind. Slowly, I pulled the beads closer, dividing my attention between the two women and the figure moving in the darkness next to Todd's fallen body.

He uncurled himself and rose. He wore orderly's clothing, but he moved with a fluid grace no mere human could match. He turned, his dark eyes fixing on Francie.

His voice, when he spoke, was deep, penetrating and hypnotic. It flowed like honey, resonating through my bones making me want, desperately, to please him. The cross began to heat, glowing bright between my clasped fingers. The pain brought me to myself, and I shuddered at the knowledge that I could not stand against this creature. He would do whatever he chose to me. But I was beneath his notice, his whole focus on the woman who stood across the hall from me.

"I want you, Francie. And I *will* have you."

"I'll kill you first." Francie's voice sounded harsh and cold.

The creature smiled with evil amusement. "You can try, perhaps you'll even succeed. But I don't think you can kill your own sister. No, I don't think you'll kill Meggie." He ran his tongue over delicately pointed fangs to get the last drops of Todd's blood.

"You *bastard*."

He moved toward her, flowing like liquid out of the dark. "You're already changing, Francie. When Meg gives you the final bite you will feel the hunger, the need. Your powers will start to manifest. But it will take your first true feeding before you are one of us, before you become immortal." His dark stare caught hers, and she stood, trapped by his gaze like a rabbit before a snake.

Meg moved in a blur of awkward speed, slamming her sister against the far side of the hallway. They fell to the floor with a sickening thud, rolling, fighting.

With no time to think, I scrabbled across the floor, throwing the rosary beads over Margaret's head as she reared back to strike.

A flash of blinding light lit the air, and the stench of crisping flesh stung my nostrils. The hallway filled with billowing smoke. My lungs burned. I coughed uncontrollably.

The cough led him to me through the smoke and hellish half-light. He fell on me like a raging beast, filled with fury and rage.

His strength was beyond belief. A backhand slap lifted me from the floor and sent me flying into the opposite side of the hallway. My head slammed painfully against the tile, and I saw the flash of stars before my vision dimmed.

Pain woke me. I lay in a growing puddle of blood and ash-fouled water. The overhead sprinkler system rained gently down on the smoking hulk;

all that remained of Margaret Coughlin. Beside her, the creature lay still on the floor, dead. My strength drained away with the blood pouring from the wound in my neck. If this was dying, it was not so very bad. Too, I did still believe in God and in heaven. My faith had not entirely deserted me.

In the distance, there were the sounds of rescuers approaching from down the hall. By the time they could reach me, it might be too late. Oddly, it didn't matter. A growing lassitude gripped me. The wet wool of my fallen coat scratched against my face, but it would be more effort than it was worth to move. All that mattered was the woman standing above the fallen creature, blouse plastered to a body wet with water and blood. Her red hair hung in thick wet clumps blocking my view of her face.

She turned, brushing the hair away. That small gesture, which should have been so human, seemed too smooth, too fluid. She turned haunting, hypnotic green eyes in my direction. From the corner of my eye, I saw a brilliant light. I turned my head fractionally to see what it could be. The rosary glowed, the metal of the crucifix bright against the charcoal mass on the floor.

Francie moved toward me in perfect, graceful slow motion. She tried to catch me with her gaze. I wouldn't look. My strength was returning. Still feeble, but growing. The near-blinding light of the cross cutting through the thinning smoke drew me, clearing my mind. Francie had nearly reached my side.

"Patrick—" her voice: honeyed sweet, so very compelling. It promised warmth, comfort. My head moved involuntarily toward that wonderful voice. The desire I experienced in that moment was out of keeping with everything I believed...everything I was. The cross flared brighter, nearly blinding me.

She hissed—not a human sound. A thrill of pure terror ran through me. I knew people were coming, but if anything, it made it worse. Unsuspecting, they would be easy prey for the thing that she would become once she'd fed.

Reverently, Francie knelt by my right side and lowered that perfect face to my wounded throat. "Just relax. You won't even remember. Your old life will be a dream you can't quite recall."

It took all of my power of will not to look at her, and I prayed for the strength to do what needed to be done. I forced my arm to move, pulling against the wet wool of my coat as the warmth of her breath whispered against the torn skin. My fingers dug into the depths of the coat pocket, probing, searching until I found what I needed.

She reared back her head to strike. I pulled my cigarette lighter from the pocket. The stabbing pain of her teeth sinking into my flesh came too late to stop me. The lighter flared to life. It turned Francie into a living, screaming torch. She burned like a gasoline soaked rag, and I felt myself burning with her, despite the water pouring down on us from the ceiling.

* * *

I wasn't able to attend Todd's funeral. I was still in the hospital with second and third degree burns, and a neck wound that wouldn't heal until I thought to clean it with holy water.

Monsignor Sheehey came to give me mass. I refused communion. I am, after all, living in a state of mortal sin. Until she took her first drink of human blood, Francie Coughlin was human. I killed her before she got that taste.

Michael Sheehey offered—hell, begged, to give me confession. After all, I can't be a priest without it. I had to turn him down.

You see, there's this little problem. I'm not sorry.

Biography

C.T. Adams and Cathy Clamp began writing as a team in 1997. They quickly learned that their individual talents in writing created a dynamite combination in historical and paranormal novels! They both reside in the Texas Hill Country where Cie lives with her dog and cats and and Cathy lives with her husband, dogs, cats and 24 Boer/Spanish cross goats! They love reading fan mail and anticipate a long and fruitful writing career.

You can visit us at our website http://www.ciecatrunpubs.com/.

Little Karen
by
Faith Bicknell-Brown

*In Appalachia, a rain crow is another word for mourning dove.

Pain comes in various guises. Harland's chose the form of a spiritual cooking lesson. It seared his soul, scorched his heart, filleted his brain, and left the taste of emptiness in his mouth. His body ached from sleep deprivation, his eyes gritty from too many tears. He wondered if eternity in Hell used the pain of loss to torment its victims.

He turned onto the lane leading to the little Cape Cod style house sorely in need of vinyl siding. A rickety garage and a brand new dog kennel stood off to the right of the dwelling. A small greenhouse presided on the opposite side of the home, every piece of glass plating smashed. The place needed a lot of work, but when Harland first followed the real estate broker out to it, he knew he would be its next owner.

The grass needed cutting. The weeping willows scattered across the wide, gently rolling lawn, spread their branches like verdant women drying their long hair. Bouncing along the rutted lane, Harland's gaze drifted over the residence. The only neatness on the scene was the new kennel and the deck built across the front of the house; the project had been completed with the help of several six-packs and Karen's keen eye for detail.

Her name blew across his mind like an unexpected breeze on a hot, still day. The pain promptly crashed through him, a bitter twist to his heart, riding on a tsunami that left carnage and destruction in its wake. He gasped, struggling with the sensation, and pulled up next to the house, shutting off the truck engine. The doctor had given him sedatives. At the moment, the thought of oblivion won the battle over pain.

He got out of the truck and started toward the deck steps. The raucous barking of the Catahoulas in the pen interrupted his purpose. Turning, he looked across the lane at the dog kennel where four females and one male jumped and yipped in anticipation.

He'd forgotten to feed them before leaving for the funeral. Harland gazed at the front door, visualizing the bottle of sedatives sitting on the kitchen counter. He looked back at the dogs wiggling from head to tail with excitement and happiness that he was home. Karen would have given him the devil for neglecting the dogs. She loved to play with them. They'd romp together in the yard, and she'd toss the ball, laughing at the antics of the two larger jips, who were both omegas, but yet had a weird affection for one another. Whenever Karen arrived, the canines cried and howled until she let them out of the pen to nuzzle and play with her.

Sighing, Harland walked to the kennel and opened the door on the far end where he stored the supplies. He filled the dog pans with food and water, locked everything up, and started toward the house. At the deck, he found St. Francis Assisi waiting for him on the railing.

"Oh, no, not you," Harland grumbled.

The rain crow looked at him with round beady black eyes; it bobbed its head in greeting.

"Karen really made a wuss out of you, bud." Harland held out his hand and the bird stepped into it. He ascended the steps and stood looking down into the unruly wildflowers that Karen had planted two months before she had died. A gazebo-shaped bird feeder hung from a wrought iron pole in the center of the flowerbed. Since spring's arrival, he had spent many mornings on the deck drinking coffee with his neighbor and watching the plethora of visiting birds. With time and diligence, Karen had coaxed two mourning doves in and eventually hand-fed them. She named the male St. Francis Assisi, but she hadn't given his mate a name since she was still too shy to approach without bribery.

He set the dove on the deck table and walked inside, tears slipping through his five o'clock shadow, eroding scars of agony into his face.

***

Sunshine blazed through the window of the loft bedroom. Harland opened his eyes, wincing against the glare. He lay there for a moment, thinking that coffee would taste great with a toasted egg, bacon and mayo sandwich. Swinging his feet over the bedside, he blearily regarded the crisscross pattern of the sunshine on the dark blue carpet. He looked through the cerulean sheers and saw a matching sky.

Downstairs, he strode through the quiet house. Karen must have had to work over at the nursing home. The only time she didn't slip into the house and make breakfast for them was when she had to fill in for someone or work a double shift, which wasn't often. He burst into the kitchen ready to jokingly chastise her for shirking her neighborly duty, but saw the sink stacked high with dirty dishes and clutter over every flat surface. He stopped cold.

Karen was dead.

He'd never enjoy another pot of her jump-start-the-dead coffee. She'd never make another toasted sandwich or her famous cinnamon rolls for their breakfast. No more would Karen's chatter fill this room, nor would her child-like giggles send pleasure through his heart.

He noticed the prescription bottle on the counter, a harbinger of dreams, addictions and denial. Its contents promised that he could forget her. Rage ripped through him. He snatched up the bottle and threw it so hard that it struck the china cabinet across the room and exploded in a shower of tiny pink pills that bounced around the kitchen.

Oblivion was the mother of cruelty. Reality's arrival mocked him. Death was their offspring, a daughter bearing misery.

A knock echoed throughout the house. Slowly, Harland made his way to the front door and opened it to find Karen's sister, Shay.

"Harland, I know this isn't a good time, but Karen left a note in the rough draft of her will that Grandma's butterfly charm might be found in a flowerbed here. Do you mind if I look for it?"

He stood looking at Shay, noting that although she favored Karen in looks, she was quite different. "Yeah, sure. Good luck. We've searched for it several times once she realized it had broken loose from the chain, but maybe you'll chance upon it."

The woman smiled uncertainly and turned, descending the deck steps. He watched as she crawled on her hands and knees through Black-eyed Susans, bachelor buttons, sweet peas, and dinner plate zinnias. The charm had been made by someone in their family during the early 1700s. It had been passed down from eldest daughter to eldest daughter. Karen slipped it off one day so he could examine it. A cluster of silver, gold, and rose gold butterflies surrounded a large teardrop-shaped opal. He didn't know much about jewelry, but he knew enough that the piece was unique. The artisan who had made it had been incredibly talented. The day Karen discovered it was missing, she had planted the flowerbed. Once she realized she'd lost it, that it was most likely buried in the dirt somewhere, she'd cried her eyes out and sulked for a week after her family had angrily ridiculed her for her carelessness.

Turning, Harland went inside and attempted to fix a pot of coffee that would strip varnish off a table and make Karen proud of him. Half an hour later, Shay stepped inside covered in soil and grass stains and reported that she'd had no luck finding the charm. She left, the sound of her car fading until all that remained were the slurps Harland created with his coffee cup.

He sat staring at the pattern in the oak tabletop. Finally, he placed his head on his folded arms and he shut his eyes.

Little Karen

* * *

"Come tell me what you think of the mailbox!" Karen waved her arms over her head catching Harland's attention. He shut off the weed whacker. "Come see what I painted on your mailbox," she called to him.

He strode to the metal mailbox and surveyed the Catahoulas that she had painted on its sides. "Wow, Karen, those look so real!"

She beamed at him, the smile lighting up her green eyes like two fiery emeralds. His heart flip-flopped and he wished that he had enough guts to kiss her, to ask his best friend to marry him. Soon he would manage enough courage to ask her, but today, they were working together, enjoying the clear weather, and laughing at one another's silly jokes.

"The banks look nice," she said, gesturing toward the slopes along the entrance of the lane. "Those briars always remind me of someone who needs a haircut."

Harland laughed. "Yeah, I guess they do." He pulled his goggles back over his eyes. "I better get back to work. I'm almost finished."

She nodded. "I'll gather up my paint supplies, and then we'll have some lunch. I brought over some pickle and cream cheese sandwiches."

"Mmm, sounds great."

Giggling like a little girl, she said, "Well, it still amazes me that you like them. Until I met you, I had never met another person who could stand pickle and cream cheese sandwiches."

He stuck his tongue out at her, starting up the weed whacker.

The trimmer's loud chainsaw-like wail drowned out all sounds. He watched the briars fall away from the whipping string. As if from a nightmare, Karen's smashed and bloody body struck the bank in front of him. At first, his mind didn't comprehend what he saw. He turned just in time to see a runaway logging truck flash past him and plow into the trees at the side of the drive. The sound of wrenching metal filled the air, dirt and tree limbs flying everywhere as if a bomb had detonated. His gaze traveled to where the mailbox used to stand, then back to Karen's inert and mangled body.

Harland awoke screaming, "NO!"

He gaped at the tabletop, the dirty dishes in the sink, the oak cupboards, and red enamel appliances. His pulse raced, his heart slamming painfully.

His anguished sobs filled the house.

* * *

He finally got a grip on himself and took his cold cup of coffee out on the deck. He sat at the table watching the wildflowers bob in the breeze like curtseying ladies. He couldn't live like this, couldn't deal with the constant pain that his best friend, the woman he loved more than anything, would never again grace him with her presence.

St. Francis Assisi flew from an electric wire and landed on the table with a bounce. He bobbed his head, sitting quietly, his dark eyes regarding Harland with curiosity.

"Where's your love?" Harland asked the rain crow, realizing the irony of his statement. His gaze scanned the yard. He spotted the female waddling through the wildflowers. "Ah, still more chicken than dove, I see."

The male cooed in agreement.

The Catahoulas began barking. The two omega females jumped across one another's backs, their excited cries escalating. The other three dogs ran in circles howling and wagging their tails.

Frowning, Harland got up and crossed the deck. He peered across the lane. Damn, he hadn't fed the dogs again. Some breeder he had become.

He crossed the property to the kennel and discovered food and water already in the dogs' pans. He knew he hadn't fed and watered them, but remembered that Shay had arrived earlier. She must've fed the dogs for him. No, she didn't know where the spare key to the storage door was kept—unless Karen had told her in the event of an emergency.

He let the dogs out to run. All five of them raced across the lane to the large yard where they had always played with Karen. They milled around, looking confused.

"Yeah, I know the feeling well, gang," Harland whispered as he returned to the deck and sat down.

He observed the dogs sniffing the willow trees, running back and forth as if disoriented. The female mourning dove shot out of the wildflowers like a cannonball, her hysterical, high-pitched cries echoing across the lawn. She set upon the electric wire, staring down with accusing eyes.

"What's wrong with your girlfriend?" Harland asked St. Francis Assisi.

The dogs began barking again, playing like they once did with Karen.

Moments later, the female rain crow glided down from her high perch and landed in the flowerbed. She scratched vigorously, flapped her wings again, and rose with a flutter to alight on the deck rail with something in her mouth. She hopped from the railing to the tabletop and landed like a feathery rubber ball.

In her beak and covered in soil, Karen's butterfly charm dangled. Harland

Little Karen

held out his hand. The mourning dove regarded him for a moment, waddled over, and politely dropped it into his palm.

"Thank you... Little Karen."

The Violin's Cry
by
Faith Bicknell-Brown

The vague opening in the trees looked more like a place where livestock had pushed through the brush than the entrance to a private drive. The fellow who owned the only gas station in Quinwood had given Dawn instructions to find Buddy Alljoy's place, but his landmarks to watch for were minor ones. She was somewhere on the eastern side of Snow Mountain, no one around for miles, smack in the middle of southern West Virginia.

The squealing brakes shattered the quiet. She flipped the automatic 4x4 switch and turned left onto the narrow path. Within seconds of turning onto the road, Dawn realized that she needed a tank instead of a truck. As she fiddled with the radio, the tires hit a rut that jarred her—hard. She quickly returned her attention to the road, grasping the steering wheel with both hands.

Wild laurel and multi flora rose bushes screeched along the vehicle's new paint. Rounding a bend overhung with tree branches, she slowed the truck to a crawl, sloshing through low places so full of water Dawn feared it would leak through the doors. If she didn't know better, she'd swear that the road was actually an old mudslide track used for a driveway.

Born and raised in the Appalachians, the majority of Dawn's thirty years were spent living along the Ohio River. She wasn't sure what to expect when she reached the Alljoy's homestead. Her neighbor had returned from his vacation with a stunning handcrafted violin that he had purchased at a flea market in Rainelle. Buddy Alljoy's name and phone number were meticulously etched on the inside behind the strings. As a journalist for one of Marietta's small newspapers, Dawn also freelanced and landed an assignment for a travel magazine. The publication had offered to pay her expenses for the research of Alljoy's story.

The Chevy came to a stop in someone's yard next to an Alice Chalmers tractor. A gangly man lifted himself out of a rusty chair upon the cluttered porch. Dawn grabbed her notebook, camera, and micro recorder.

"Hello, Mr. Alljoy!" Dawn called, waving.

"Ma'am." He yanked open the screen. "Dad, that writer lady from Ohio is here!" He turned and favored her with a gap-toothed smile. "I'm George Alljoy, Buddy's son. I won't be stayin', ma'am, I promised my wife I'd help her pick tomatoes."

"I'm sorry, I thought you were Buddy."

"Hell, don't make no difference who you're talkin' to 'cause everyone's related on this mountain. If you tell the wrong feller it'll get around to the right one eventually."

Embarrassed, she sighed and blew a lock of blonde hair out of her eyes. She dodged several mongrels milling around the yard and climbed the porch steps.

The clapboard house desperately needed a paint job. Inside, a menagerie of spiritual pictures and icons cluttered the dwelling. Perched upon a bookshelf stuffed with paperbacks, a thirteen-inch color television blasted an episode of Wheel of Fortune. On the left, bright ceiling lights illuminated a large kitchen, and a curtained doorway loomed in the far right corner. Scuffed gray linoleum covered the floor. Mortared flagstones shouldered a coal stove that squatted in the opposite corner like a great iron toad.

A much older version of George Alljoy emerged through the curtain, pushing a shriveled old woman in a wheelchair. The old-timer seemed both pleased and embarrassed with Dawn's presence. He wheeled the elderly woman next to the television and paused to turn down the volume.

He offered his long-fingered hand. "Name's Buddy Alljoy." His firm, dry grip nearly brought tears to Dawn's eyes. "So you think people are gonna want to read about me?"

"I sure do." Immediately, Dawn knew she liked the man. "You'll be surprised how far out of their way some collectors will go to find something unique." Her gaze drifted to the crippled woman staring blankly at the game show. "May I see some of your work?"

"Really?" Buddy grinned at her, revealing the absence of bottom teeth.

"You mentioned on the phone that you have a very nice one made out of cherry." Dawn noted the drool that oozed out of the old woman's mouth and onto the bib tied around her neck. She restrained the urge to walk over and wipe her chin.

Buddy moved toward the curtained door. "Can't. Sold that one Sunday night to the preacher for a hundred bucks."

Dawn blinked.

"I have three others finished and two I'm workin' on. Give me a sec..."

Dawn couldn't restrain herself any longer. Whether or not Buddy got upset didn't matter. She couldn't stand watching the spittle drip off the elderly woman's chin. Gently wiping the woman's mouth clean, Dawn glanced over her shoulder and found Buddy watching her from the doorway.

"That's Mabel, my wife. She had a stroke a li'l over a year ago and has been that way ever since."

Gibberish burst from Mabel, her head jerking to the left.

Concerned, Dawn leaned over her. "I take it she can't talk?"

"Nope, just makes the occasional noise or a high-pitched squeal. Doctor says that she isn't aware of anything. Said that the stroke did extensive damage, so she's more or less just a vegetable now."

Buddy sat down on the threadbare sofa, clutching a violin in each hand. The gloss on the instruments glimmered in the dim illumination of the overhead bulb. He motioned for Dawn to have a seat.

"This here is the first violin I ever made." He offered it to Dawn.

It frightened her to touch such a beautiful labor of love. The violin's smooth light-colored, highly polished surface reflected images around the room. The obvious care and work involved in the instrument's construction filled her with awe.

"You said that you sold the cherry violin for one hundred dollars?"

The old man nodded. "Yep, for Mabel's last prescription 'cause we didn't have the money." He caressed the violin's side as if it were a child's brow. "The preacher's boy loved its perdy red wood. Boy has a true ear for music, though, and is a good match for that instrument.

"Medicare doesn't help much with Mabel's medicines," Buddy turned Mabel's wheelchair around so that she faced them, "so this talent the Good Lord gave me comes in handy in a pinch."

Mabel gurgled, one hand twitching before it grew still again.

Dawn returned the violin to Buddy's sure hands. She took her micro recorder out of her pocket and turned it on.

"Buddy, do you realize that you have the means to make things easier financially for you and your wife?"

The old man stared at her.

"You can make a decent living by crafting your violins," she said, chuckling.

"I always thought it was just a convenient way to make a few extra bucks when we needed it."

Smiling, Dawn replied, "After this article about you and your violins is published, you'll be able to set your price."

Through the entire interview with Buddy, which had Dawn in stitches from his amusing life stories, Mabel gurgled and grew agitated. Buddy repeatedly cleaned her chin. The old woman's hands twitched, her head occasionally jerking to the left.

"Is something causing her to do that? I mean, aside from what's normal for her now since the stroke?" Dawn stood out of the way as Buddy prepared Mabel to sit with them on the porch where they planned to enjoy the cool evening.

"She does that sometimes." Buddy retrieved an earthen jug from a kitchen cupboard. "Her doctor says that those fits are to be expected after a massive stroke and that the human brain is a mystery, so there's no tellin' why she really does certain things."

Frowning, Dawn followed him as he wheeled Mabel outside. She really hadn't known what to expect before she met the Alljoy's, but she felt bad for her ignorant misconceptions of mountain folk. What reason could there be for such a terrible thing to happen to such lovely people? Her heart went out to Buddy and his wife.

The evening air soughed around the corner of the house. Buddy set the brake on the wheelchair and poured two cups from the jug. The sip of stump liquor whispered down Dawn's throat; it bloomed in her stomach and sent a heat spreading through her body that urged a sweat to break out along her skin.

"That's smooth stuff!" Dawn gasped and sat back. She listened to a whippoorwill behind the house. Watching an orange barn cat groom itself on the tractor seat, she knew that she really should be heading back to the motel, but it was so nice to enjoy the beauty of the mountain evening and the Alljoy's company. Life here was simple but in other ways more complex. Her short time with Buddy and Mabel had taught her so much.

Buddy's rocking chair creaked as he rocked. "Mabel used to make the best dandelion wine in these parts." He refilled his cup.

"Were there any warning signs before the stroke?" Dawn observed Mabel's head jerk to one side, as if she were trying to turn toward her voice.

"Nope." Buddy shook his head sadly. "Mabel was always healthy as a horse, hardly ever got a cold."

The old woman uttered an odd squeal.

Startled, Dawn leaned close and peered intently into the woman's distorted face. A warm brown gaze briefly met Dawn's. Something flashed in Mabel's eyes, something so fleeting, so minute that Dawn wondered if she'd truly seen it, or if the woman's eyes had caught the reflection of an evening star. Mabel rolled to the side as if something interesting hung in midair and remained there.

"I think the hardest thing for me," Buddy looked at Dawn, "is that I can't talk to her anymore." He glanced down at his feet, now avoiding Dawn's gaze. "Mabel and me endured things that would break most of today's relationships." Buddy's lower lip trembled. "I don't mind taking care of Mabel. Lord knows she was always there for me, but I miss our talks we used to have out here on warm evenings.

"During the cold months we'd move close to the coal burner with some 'shine or coffee. Whenever she was upset or had a bad day, all I had to do was play my violin for her. Mabel said I was the only one who could make a violin weep so perdy."

Dawn's throat constricted. This certainly was not how she expected her interview to end. She placed her hand over Mabel's. The woman's fingers twitched. Again, she met the old woman's earthy gaze, and for an instant, caught a glimpse of the person inside her maimed body.

The most unexpected and intense emotion surged through Dawn. She blurted her words before she realized it. "Buddy, I think Mabel would like you to play for her now."

The old man sighed. "I don't play no more 'cept to tune an instrument when I string 'em."

Dawn gazed at Mabel and knew that his beloved wife was trapped in a useless prison. "Maybe you should favor your gal with a tune, Buddy."

Sighing, he relented. "All right." Buddy swiped at his eyes with the back of his hand and stepped inside the house. Minutes later, he returned with one of the newly finished instruments.

As he tuned the violin, evening settled around the mountain. The sunset's blazing pinks and purples melded with the navy of night. Somewhere a bobcat screeched. The mutts dozing on the porch steps perked their ears, but didn't move.

By the meager light, Buddy began to play. Dawn didn't recognize the melody, the notes soulful and melancholy. Mabel's head jerked toward her husband, her eyes rolling from side to side, her inability to focus on him obviously distressing her.

A ghostly sound erupted from Mabel. Her hands twitched in a repetitive manner. The notes bursting from the violin transformed into pure emotion as if the instrument wept, mourning a lost love and Mabel's cry echoed it. Her sounds grew louder, briefly matching the violin's note for note. The tune ended, and Buddy laid the instrument across his lap, taking his wife's hands into his own.

He reached up and gently wiped away a tear that sparkled upon her cheek.

"It's good to have you back, Mabel." Buddy leaned forward and brushed her lips with his own. "Forgive me for not looking closer. Forgive me for listening to those know-nothing doctors!"

Again, Mabel's cry echoed the violin's. It drifted upon the night breeze, traveling across the Appalachians to wherever answered prayers reside.

The 63rd President
by
Faith Bicknell-Brown

His birth certificate lay inside a small cedar box. Beyond his parents, Marshall's knowledge of his family consisted of a penknife that supposedly belonged to his grandfather, the initials MC carved into its ivory handle. The remainders of the box's contents were a pink geode, some useless coins and a two-dollar bill. Marshall shut the lid, shoving the container under his cot.

Thinking about the lost time capsule, Marshall realized his cedar box was a time capsule too. After the invasion occurred forty-four years ago, his mother had given Marshall the box, putting him in Pap's care. Pap took him, fleeing with the others, but Marshall's mother stayed in hopes of convincing her husband to escape with them. Marshall never saw either of his parents again. His only link to the past resided in the small chest.

The tent flap opened, and Pap shuffled inside.

"Can't stand that sun!" The elderly fellow lowered himself onto his makeshift bed. "I think my brain's been baked into mush!"

"Your brain has always been mushy, Pap," Marshall said, slipping on his boots.

"Thanks for clearing that up." Pap's eyes sparkled with amusement. "Jazz says that they think they found the time capsule. Everyone's waiting for you at the dig site. They want you to open it."

Marshall bolted out of the tent.

By the time he reached the dig, sweat trickled freely through his hair. He quickly climbed down into the pit where his colleagues sat around a shallow hole.

"Pap told me the news!" Marshall said, panting. "Is it the real thing this time?"

Jazz glanced up, her gold eyes full of excitement. "Looks like the time capsule all right." Pulling a tarpaulin off a large metal trunk, she said, "It fits the description of the handwritten records."

"I'd given up on finding it," Marshall said softly.

"We broke the lock, but haven't lifted the lid yet." Jazz grinned, faint crow's feet appearing around her eyes. "Everyone agreed that you should be the one to look inside first."

Marshall hopped down into the shallow hole. At first, the lid proved stubborn, but after he yanked on it several times, it came loose with a screech and a puff of stale dust. A menagerie of strange items lay inside the chest.

Carefully picking up a rolled document, Marshall opened it. "It's the letter signed by the mayor before the invasion started," he said to everyone.

A photo had been inserted inside the letter. He studied the picture of a young boy clad only in jeans, sitting in front of a red, white and blue flag.

For some reason, the boy seemed very familiar.

* * *

Quiet permeated the tiny archeological community. The crew had retired for the night, but Marshall sat in his tent, examining the items found at the site. He kept returning to the picture of the boy in front of the American flag.

"When you discover the meaning of our crappy existence in that photograph, put that dang light out and go to bed," Pap grumbled from his cot.

"I'm sorry, Pap." Marshall glanced at his guardian. "But there's something so familiar about this picture, like I should know this kid, or maybe what he's doing there."

Pap sighed and rolled over, facing Marshall. "I promised your mother I'd take care of you, but that didn't mean I had to put up with your shit at two in the morning!"

"Okay!" Marshall tossed the picture down. "I'll shut off the damn light!" He blew out the candles and stomped over to the tent opening.

"Marshall?"

Pausing at the flap, Marshall waited.

"I'm sorry, boy." A sigh filled the tent. "You'll find your answer in that picture if you look hard enough."

"You really think so?" Marshall asked.

Pap laughed softly, but said nothing.

Marshall shook his head, stepping out of the tent. He followed a footpath to a jumble of boulders behind the tent community. Climbing, he reached the top. He found a comfortable spot and sat watching the moonlight upon Lake Erie's gentle waves. After the war, Earth's population had dropped by two-thirds, and nearly every historical record had been eradicated. Once the aliens had depleted most of Earth's resources, they left intent on doing the same to the next inhabitable world. Looking at the silhouettes of wreckage, Marshall wondered what Cleveland must have looked like perched upon the shoreline.

"Pap said I would find you up here."

The 63rd President

Startled, Marshall looked up at Jazz.

She grinned and sat down. Handing him the photo of the boy, she said, "Pap nearly ripped my head off when I stopped by to see if you were awake." Laughing throatily, Jazz added, "Anyway, he said for me to give that picture to you." She quickly built a fire out of wood scraps and trash. From her over-sized trousers, she withdrew a crude slingshot and squatted next to the dancing flames. Poised with the little weapon, she waited.

"Mmm, hmm," Marshall said absently, his attention fixating on the photograph.

Jazz asked, "What's with you? Ever since you found that photo, you've been acting weird." A rodent scurried into their ring of firelight; she let a rock fly, whooping when it struck her quarry.

"It's like I should know who this kid is and why he was there." Marshall leaned back, resting on one elbow. "Pap says I'll find all the answers to my questions in this photograph."

"Aw, hell, Pap always talks in riddles!" Hurrying down the rock, Jazz snatched up the quivering rat. She bit into its neck, sucking it dry of all fluids. Finished, she turned and looked at Marshall. He gulped, hoping he didn't vomit in front of her. "I didn't have much time to eat today. I was so hungry, I just didn't think."

Marshall swallowed his bile. "That's okay."

Jazz returned to her seat and wiped the animal's blood from her mouth. "You lament the fact that you know nothing of your family except what Pap has told you about your parents. It could be worse, Marshall. You could've had my alien father with the knowledge you were born from a violent rape."

Snorting, Marshall glanced over at her. "You have an interesting way of looking at things."

She shrugged. "Would you like to trade places?"

His gaze fell upon the drained rodent. "No."

"I didn't think so."

The edges of the photo kept curling. Leaning toward the dying fire, Marshall peered at the top right corner and found a crescent mark on the edge. He pinched it. A bright flash startled him and he dropped the picture.

Like an old film projector, a light beam erupted from the photo's center. A lifelike American flag with the young boy reclining in front of it appeared a few feet in front of them. Words glowed at the bottom of the vivid projection.

"What's that writing say?" Jazz whispered.

Softly, Marshall read the writing. "Marshall Carson, age twelve. Photo taken by his mother, Doris Carson, at the Fourth of July Festival held in Cleveland, Ohio. Marshall Carson later graduated from Harvard, launching a promising career in adapting alien technology to various American Government projects. He married at age thirty, fathering two children before his interest in politics prompted him to run for Ohio Senator, then governor. Eight years later, Marshall Carson became the sixty-third United States President."

The picture wavered like ripples upon water and faded. Blinking, Marshall questioned what he had just read. Gently, he picked up the photograph.

"What's does that mean?" Jazz fixed him with a penetrating gaze.

"Dunno, but I'm going to find out."

* * *

"I swear, Marshall, I got more rest when we were still fighting those damn aliens!" Pap rubbed the sleep from his eyes.

Marshall set a burning candle on a tiny bed table. He shoved the picture under Pap's nose. "Who's that boy in the photograph?"

Glancing over at Jazz, Pap raised his fuzzy white eyebrows in a defeated expression. "Found out about the picture, did he?"

Jazz grinned.

"Quit playing games, Pap!" Marshall flipped the picture onto the bed covers. Turning, he pulled the cedar box out from under his cot and withdrew his birth certificate. "Why does that boy have the same name as mine?"

With a groan, Pap swung his feet over the cot's side. He studied the intense expression upon his ward's face. Marshall looked back, his gaze steady.

"That boy was your grandfather."

"My grandfather was the sixty-third President of the United States?" Marshall said.

"Yes, he was in office when the invasion happened. He was used as an example and executed on television in front of millions. It was the aliens' way of showing what would happen to Humankind if anyone resisted." Pap sighed, gesturing at Jazz to sit down.

Marshall realized his guardian was serious. "Why didn't you tell me? Why keep my grandfather's identity a secret?"

"Why bother until the need arose?" Pap stood, grasping his ward's shoulder. "If you discovered the time capsule with the picture, and figured out the boy's identity in the photo, then the news would spread." He waved one gnarled hand, indicating their tiny camp. "And believe me, it will! People will look to you for leadership, boy. You are the grandson of the last American President." He handed Marshall the picture. "I told you only what was necessary because it's easier for you to believe your heritage when you discover it on your own. If you didn't find the capsule, then there was no harm done."

"You probably wouldn't have truly comprehended the implications if he had told you long ago," Jazz added softly.

Marshall nodded, staring at the photo. "I understand now." He took the penknife from the box and slipped it into his pocket.

"Thank God!" Pap lay back down and snatched the covers up over his head.

Jazz walked to the tent flap. "Ya know, Marshall," she said, turning. "You're about to give everyone something they've never had before."

Shutting the box, Marshall set it on the table. "What's that?"

"Hope." She smiled and stepped out into the darkness.

Uncle Willy's Cure
by
Faith Bicknell-Brown

Spanish moss hung from the large oak trees and provided shade for the small stone church. Victoria shooed a fly away from her brother's wheelchair. She listened to their parents discuss plans for visiting the mission and the Fountain of Youth.

Hot and bored, William tugged on his sister's hand. "Vic, I want to see the fountain first."

Victoria nodded, stooped, and swatted sand from her petticoats. She watched her mother spin her lace parasol as Papa mulled over the park map.

"Vic, tell Mama I'm hot."

She glanced at her brother's liver-spotted hand on her skirt. Her gaze traveled to the ancient face, which cloaked the ten-year-old child behind it. She smiled into his eyes, the only evidence of his true age.

"Try to be patient, Willy, you know how Papa and Mama are about plans, money, and worship." She pulled a lace fan out of her skirt pocket and waved it next to her brother's face.

"I know," William sighed. "But it means we'll be here all day. Are we staying in St. Augustine tonight?"

"I don't know." She shrugged. "Mama," Victoria called hesitantly. "William is terribly hot. Is it all right if I take him to the fountain now? You know how the heat weakens him."

Mama glanced around the lacey pink parasol, her cool blue eyes vaguely irritated. She looked at Papa, who seemed totally absorbed in the map, and said something quietly. Papa nodded.

"Papa is torn between whether to start at the sanctuary or the cemetery." Mama's skirts stirred up sand as she strolled toward them, spinning her parasol. "I believe that a cool drink from the fountain would be nice. I think," she sobered as two elderly matrons walked by on their way to the church, "that *Uncle Willy* needs a reward for his patience."

William looked up at his sister and rolled his eyes.

Victoria ignored him, and with the elderly tourists still within earshot, carefully chose her next words. "I think *Uncle Willy* is more interested in a cure."

Mama laughed softly and waited for Victoria to release the wheelchair's brake. Victoria noted how her mother's trained eyes watched for any sign that William might tumble from his seat while she labored with him over

Uncle Willy's Cure

the rough ground.

The long line of people waiting at the entrance of the springhouse caused Mama to cluck her tongue in irritation.

"Oh, how vexing!" Mama placed one hand on her daughter's elbow. "Let us return to the church. The line is long and *Uncle Willy's* wheelchair won't fit through the doorway."

"You go back, Mama. I'll stay with him and fetch a cup of water when it's our turn." Victoria sensed her brother's urgency and set her face into the most mature expression that she could muster in hopes that their mother would relent.

A genuine smile graced Mama's lips. "If you insist, Victoria. Try not to be gone too long. Papa will have kittens if his schedule is knocked askew." Without a backward glance, she left the children.

"Do you think the water will make me young again, Vic?"

The look of intense hope in her brother's eyes sent a pain through Victoria's heart. Locked inside the useless, decaying prison of his body, Willy deserved something special to brighten his life. Fear stirred within Victoria like an unborn embryo. Fear of the death, which loomed over him. Fear that she would develop the same strange condition.

"I know that you want to believe that it will." She used a linen hanky to wipe a trickle of sweat from William's temple. "Maybe if you truly believe..." She shrugged.

Gradually the tourists dispersed. William looked around, his head wobbling on his frail neck.

"Where did everyone go?"

His sister surveyed the surrounding paths and the adjacent cemetery. Park visitors began gathering upon blankets spread under the best shade trees and opened bountiful picnic baskets. She glanced at the sun through the twisted live oaks draped in Spanish moss.

"I'm guessing that it's the supper hour, Willy."

"May I be of some assistance to you youngsters?"

Victoria turned to regard a small, wizened gentleman with an engaging grin on his sun-browned face. He studied them with eyes that looked like two almond-shaped onyxes that left an unsettled sensation in Victoria's stomach. She looked hard, trying to discern their pupils. His grin widened and his head bobbed from side to side, reminding her of a curious gecko she once saw when they visited Mama's eldest sister in New Mexico.

"I want a drink from the fountain, but my wheelchair won't fit through the door," William piped up regardless of his sister's warning look.

"I'm the caretaker of the fountain," the old man said congenially. "If you wish, I will carry you inside."

"Really?" The smile on William's face could have melted the Devil's heart.

"Uncle Willy, I don't think—"

"If the young lady feels it's all right." The caretaker fixed Victoria with his penetrating gaze.

Although the man unnerved her, something about him counteracted her unease. The combination of the two sensations left her confused. She relented at the delighted expression on her brother's face.

"Very well."

"Oh, thank you, Vic!"

The caretaker placed a hand upon her shoulder and squeezed gently. "You are a fine sister."

"Oh, but he's my Uncle..." Victoria's lips refused to form the rest of her denial. Somehow the old man knew the truth—but how?

The caretaker scooped her brother from the wheelchair, ducking through the low entrance.

"Will the water make me look like I'm a little boy?" William's head lolled against the old gent's shoulder, too weak to hold it at an angle.

"It depends."

"Depends upon what?" Victoria sat down on the low stone wall constructed around the fountain. The cool air of the springhouse soothed her sweaty brow. Water cascaded from a small jumble of rocks, trickled into a shallow pool, and disappeared into a crack in the back wall.

"It depends upon the person. Depends upon their heart, their willingness to believe, and their needs." With William on his lap, the caretaker sat down next to Victoria, holding the boy as if he were a large baby.

"I have a strange ailment." William snuggled into the old man's arms, utterly content. "Mama says that we have to tell everyone that I'm an old uncle so that people won't treat me bad or feel sorry for me."

"Or be frightened of you?" the elderly man added.

Slowly, cautiously, William nodded.

"You have what will one day be called Hutchinson-Gilford Progeria Syndrome." The caretaker turned the boy carefully on his lap so that he could see into the pool. "There won't be a cure until the year 2123, but you are lucky to have come to the fountain."

"How do you know all this? No disrespect, sir, but you seem to be just a lonely old man telling stories." Victoria smoothed her voluminous skirts and glanced into the pool. Her mouth went dry, and her heart palpitated in her chest.

Uncle Willy's Cure

The old man grinned at her, but his reflection in the spring revealed a small gray creature. Its large bulbous head seemed disproportionate to the rest of its delicate body. Enormous solid black eyes stared back at her unblinkingly.

She gaped at him. Didn't William see the same thing?

"What's your name?" William asked as he gazed into the pool.

"Ponce De Leon."

Victoria's mind raced. Along with all of Mama's schooling, she also taught her history. Could this old man be the same person?

"Mama says that you died from a battle wound after you returned to your ship," she said softly.

"That is but a story. I had sipped from the pool before I left St. Augustine, so I've been here now for many centuries. The alien civilization that settled here first were the Timucua Indians. They warned me of this fountain, but I didn't listen." He smiled. "The only way you can see what you become after drinking from it is to look at your reflection in this pool."

William's head slowly turned to lean against the man's breast. "I bet this fountain is why the Timucua refused to be Christians at first."

The old man smiled. "You are a very wise young man. The Timucua converted to more easily assimilate the newcomers into their society. Once the Europeans realized the Timucua's true identity, it was too late."

"So there are others, right?" Fearing the answer, Victoria still desired to know it.

"Yes. There are thousands upon thousands of us now. Each one who drinks from the fountain becomes one of us."

"What about William?" she asked.

"I don't want to die like this, Vic." William stared at her, his expression pleading. "I don't know why I have this condition, but it's not fair that I do." He tugged gently on Ponce De Leon's shirt. "Do you think God is punishing me because I accidentally killed Mama's cat with my slingshot?"

"You shot Cotton?" Victoria blurted. "Mama blamed Andrew Mills next door. No wonder Mrs. Mills is so angry with Mama!"

The old gent chuckled. "There could be any number of reasons, William, or no reason at all. This is but one of many strange worlds."

"I want a drink."

Victoria felt that she should stop him, but her mouth wouldn't work. William was right about the unfairness of his ailment. He was just a ten-year-old child. He deserved a normal life—or something equivalent to one.

Ponce De Leon picked up the wooden ladle on the wall's rim, stooped slightly with William in his lap, and scooped out a cup of water. He held it to the boy's lips, and William drank greedily.

Finished, William sighed. "That was good and very cold."

"Do you want me to sit you in your chair?" Ponce De Leon asked.

"No, I'd like to sit here before people return, if you don't mind," William replied.

"Very well." Ponce De Leon took Victoria's hand. "Take care of your brother. He is special." He positioned William against his sister and left quietly, a satisfied smile upon his face.

"William, did you see anything strange in the pool's reflection?"

"No."

"Nothing at all?"

"Just the three of us." William laced his fingers through hers. "Why?"

"Oh, nothing. I guess I'm tired."

A young couple entered the springhouse and sampled the water. They bid them farewell and followed the graveled path out the back door.

"We better get back to Papa and Mama," Victoria suggested. "Folks are starting to return." She used the ladle to get a drink, feeling ludicrous about the entire visit with the story-telling old man. After a long cooling swallow, she set the ladle on the wall.

"Are you ready?"

"Yes."

"Let me get your arm across my shoulder and I'll help you to your wheelchair."

"No, I think I'll walk."

"Walk?" Surprise coursed through Victoria. "Are you serious?"

"I suddenly feel strong enough to walk a few steps." Slowly, William got to his feet.

Reluctantly, Victoria stared into the fountain pool, her scream lodging tightly in her throat. There, in the water's reflection, she saw two small, gray creatures with huge, dark eyes. One wore a dress just like hers, and the other wore Willy's clothes. Her gaze shifted to her brother.

He grinned back at her, his face that of a real ten-year-old boy's. "Remember, he said that the truth is only seen in the fountain's reflection."

Collecting Data
by
Faith Bicknell-Brown

(Previously published in Would That It Were.com)

The executioner wiped the guillotine blade and motioned for the next sentencing to begin. Denise observed from behind the gallows, marveling at the senselessness of death. There was no use for her to feel pity for these people; she was here to perform her duty.

The townspeople packed themselves tightly together, moving toward the gallows, desiring a closer view of their doomed monarch. The guards exited the prison and marched the sobbing woman up the gallows steps.

Denise didn't dare shake her head in sympathy, or the throng of people would be upon her like rabid dogs, and her pretension was to remain hidden. Her head joining the others in the basket would result in an aborted mission.

The crying monarch was forced to kneel, her neck placed in the notch and fastened. Hair hung in her face, her tears dripping upon the wooden planks. The richly embroidered clothes she favored had been replaced with a drab gray dress, her velvet-slippered feet now bare and dirty.

"Kill her!" a beggar woman screamed in the crowd.

Others echoed her words, the angry blood lust drifting upon the rancid air.

The warden read the woman's sentence, and the death-hungry mass cheered. The drum roll began, the blade whooshed down, and the queen's head parted from her rigid body with a wet noise. It tumbled into a gore-splattered basket. Two men lifted the corpse and carried it down to a wagon full of pateless bodies.

Yelling joyously, the crowd milled around, discussing justice, celebrating revenge. Denise observed them quietly, waiting for a servant to bring her the basket. Finally, she made her way into the prison with the heavy, gruesome load. She set it outside a door where someone would skewer the severed heads on pikes as examples.

Denise's artificial skin began itching again. She couldn't wait to shed it, allowing her own smooth, silver skin to breathe. Grimacing, she glanced down the corridor and extracted the monarch's head along with the king's. After focusing her energy on two peasant skulls, they soon represented the missing leaders. No sense in causing unnecessary suspicion.

With the hair of the pates in each hand, Denise hurried down the long passage, glad her mission was finally completed. She inspected the queen's sightless eyes. The woman had been executed for saying, "let them eat cake". There must be some power in this "cake" since it caused hate and death. It warranted further investigation, and Denise would include this in her report she presented with the specimens. It was easier to impart information from a decapitated head than by abducting the entire person. What remained in the brain played like a video when reason and emotion were absent. Discovering why humankind delighted in death and chaos was essential for future cohabiting.

When Denise reached a dark storage alcove, she sighed happily, delighted to return to the Mother Ship. With the queen's and king's heads, she disappeared in a flash of light.

Biography

Faith Bicknell-Brown's work has appeared in a wide range of genres such as: *Would That It Were, Touch Magazine, GC Magazine, Ohio Writer Magazine* (non-fiction), *Waxing and Waning* (Canada), and *The Istanbul Literature Review* (Turkey) just to name a few. She was a regular contributor to *Gent* under her pseudonym, Molly Diamond. She has also had fiction published in *Hustler's Busty Beauties, Penthouse Variations, Twenty 1 Lashes,* and has become a regular contributor to *Ruthie's Club*. In addition, Faith has several e-books and some print titles published under her newest pen names.

For two years, Faith served as the co-editor of *The Tenacity Times*. In October 2001, she took the position of romance and horror editor for *Wild Child Publishing* and now serves as the managing editor for WCP as well as its sister division, Freya's Bower.

She is represented by TriadaUS Literary Agency and is working on a romance novel.

The Beekeeper
by
James Cheetham

To be witness to a perfect sound. To grasp at one single, solitary moment of absolute perfection. Our birth, and perhaps our death. Two seconds of perpetual individualism wrapped in precision, provided by nature. Sweet those moments are. Sweet as honey on one's tongue.

The beekeeper longed for either. To be born again, or to die. His mind now softened by generations, he could no longer draw a line between the two. Instead, he traveled solo through time and space. His memories, tapestries of trial and error. His mournful stare resting on nothing particular anymore. In a moment lost, yet not so long ago, the beekeeper was life itself, in all its pleasure and pain. He was here, of this earth, bonded by temperament, and provoked each morning by the subtle warmth of the sun upon his youthful face.

In this, his past life, he learned in short time that trust was universal. His netting, his hat, his gloves permanent fixtures on a wooden coat rack upon the porch. The subjects and their hum, they softened with time, as did he. Of yellow and black, of contrast to blue and the sky that painted their background, they were slaves to their dance, bearers of the sweetest fruit as they sang their instinctual song. They were a whole in some ways. A lot like him—one single entity. The tribe of stingers and pollen-swollen legs acted as one, a unison with which the human race would never come to terms. *It would be our downfall*, the beekeeper concluded, a passing thought ripped from the void and slammed back again, a pain in the back of his skull. That was why, no matter how we lived our lives, we died alone and scared in the end.

"It's time," the Beekeeper said and struggled to raise his chin.

A shadow moved across his room and acknowledged him with a sigh. It was enough for him, his strength stolen along with his youth, the bitterness he thought settled long ago. Visions drifted between the soft fragrance of fresh grass and linen. He ran between the white sheets Mother left on the line and magnificent clouds he was certain were born the very day he inhaled that first cusp of mortal air. Substance was life at tender age and false assumption. Such security, and so far from Death's reach was childhood. So sensuous, and how very misleading it was to run with bones still soft and unbreakable.

"I was young," he whispered to the shadow.

The shadow knew this was true. The shadow glanced at the aged and

The Beekeeper

faded photos, dust-covered and unsettling. The circle of life everywhere. The carcass of a mounted snow owl, and the bitter scent of blackened fruit still in view upon the kitchen table. She was well-versed in this cycle and so sure now that the beekeeper was nearing the one thing equal to his first gasp of life giving air; his last would come before sundown. She brought him a cup of water, and he sipped at it mercilessly. She took the cup from his cracked lips, and a single drop rolled down his coffee-colored skin to dangle perpetually from white stubble, his tongue still savoring the cool paradox of his dying mouth.

"I was young..."

"I know you were," the shadow said. The sun outside gave clue to her somber face, lost as quickly in the moment. She went to the sink and dampened a cloth under cold running water.

The beekeeper closed his eyes. The shadow could not understand. A lifetime of domination over tribes, they crawled upon his arms, hovered around his ears. It took a certain mastery to avoid insanity when his subjects attempted entry. A gentle sway of a hand, and they returned to their purpose, sticky honey between thick worker fingers. He was a genteel. Cautious and assertive, he harvested his subject's accretion, and in return, they grew in strength, embraced their instinct, and accepted him amidst their steady hum. And he worked them like he worked himself. Expecting nothing less than perfection, he toiled until his youth was spent and then beyond. Then pain. Cramps crawled in his hands and up in his arms, screaming, as the beekeeper endured, and his subjects maintained the crops.

"They turned on me."

With time comes old age, and the human spirit is said to prevail even when adages are best left unspoken. Weakened bones of boys can be blamed on time. Muscles of sun-roasted steel are stolen like the kisses of little girls. Trembling hands and denial cause loss of faith. The beekeeper's subjects, at times overcome with the weakness of human trait, chose to leave tiny black stingers in their holiness' flesh, never to die alone, never an outcast from the tribe. He would pick at the swollen wound with unsteady fingers and continue on, unwilling to settle into the undeniable reality that what once was, was no longer.

The shadow crossed the room. Scent of toast followed her; scent of fruit painted her back into his reality. The beekeeper sniffed at the air. The shadow could not understand.

In the presence of the tribes of legs and hum, he contributed his lot to the human race as willingly. He raised his daughter to be proud, though voiceless, and conditioned his loving wife to his command, expecting the same obedience received from his hives to be echoed in the corridors of his own home. With the same placid hands, the beekeeper reaped his sugary crops; he ruled his own hive as well. Work fingers sore after connecting with loving flesh, the hive closed off from the rest of the world, his human subjects immersed in the confusion of dedicated love and disenchantment. There was a time he was far less willing, but now, as the seconds ticked by, he was prepared to pay any price to go back, to amend, and to explain it was the only way he knew, and in those words, it was simply that he longed only for what was best for them. A fleeting wish surrounded by fleeting thoughts.

His own father, a distant memory, another version of sting, of stain; tears that flowed like honey from the hive. Damn him and his iron hands, his fabled morals, his work ethic born and drawn from immigrant impatience. The way he made a boy miss him even after tanning his fragile pride. Father stood before the beekeeper, and then vanished amongst the sunbeams and dust.

"Didn't need him—never did."

And Mother—her auburn hair, how it tickled his cheeks, how it smelled of strawberries and cream. She was too tender, but only in hindsight. As a boy, he longed for it, and as a man, he sent it away, buried it with her ageless body, a victim of epidemic proportions at the age of twenty-three. Mother was an angel, but then she died. Why did she die?

"She didn't love me is why…"

But she did, oh how she did…

The shadow crossed behind him, wisped a cool motion upon his heated neck, and the beekeeper sighed. His tongue found the cavity where his young teeth once flourished. His hands, longing for substance, caressed the wood grain of a chair as old and worn as himself. Today was a special day. Today was absolute perfection. Through the entire life that was his own, as long in that tooth as he was, he outlived all but one molar. There was little to complain about then. He raced with death and won, his life was full and soon complete. The beekeeper, his kingdom of hives and sweet hum, his family before and beyond, humble and righteous, his mark lay in waiting now, a simple polished stone and a name. He would rest—well-deserving with minor, yes, minor regrets.

"I believe it's time," he said with forceful anticipation of action. The shadow moved next to him.

"We must dress you first."

"Then let's," he said, wanting even embedded in his regret to have the final say, the man about the house, the keeper, the speaker, and provider.

The Beekeeper

The shadow unbuckled his belt and tugged at his clothing, and chill settled in around him. The cold air licked his skin and replaced his pride.

Vulnerability overwhelmed his dresser. She let out a delicate whimper.

"Who is that crying?"

The shadow moved her face closer to his, and he opened his eyes, peering as well as he could around the blindness death sent in prior arrangements.

"It's me, Papa. It's Molly."

The stranger had tears in her eyes, tears in the crevasses that carved through her face. Her youth was not stolen yet, just drained. Slowly, methodically, like sand down a sinkhole. The stranger was sad; her eyes spoke from behind stone features.

"You better not be crying for me."

The beekeeper's legs were pulled from below him, and he was lifted roughly off his chair. A fresh pair of pants climbed back towards his pathetic waist.

"It's still about you, Papa, isn't it? It is me, can't you see that? Can't you see what I do for you?"

"It's time."

"Yes!" the woman, no longer a shadow but still so very much a stranger, cried. Her fingers wrapped tightly around the beekeeper's thin wrists. "Yes, it is time."

The beekeeper was lifted from his resting spot to a wheelchair, his body light as a feather now, his mind an eternity of emptiness, randomness, and misfire. The stranger ignored him, and his anger tightened. His fists gripped tightly at the air, and he wrestled to remember her misplaced name. She would be put in her place when it came back to him.

With his voice clear and expectant, he asked her again, "Who will tend to the hives?"

"Nobody, Papa."

"Someone must attend to the hi..."

"The hives are gone!" the stranger cried as she fixed his tie with trembling fingers. She saw the hurt in his eyes, and her heart ached as it always had. The only remnant of the innocent boy lay still, in the blue gentleness of the old man's soul. He was stubborn in his insecurities, she thought. Lost in a past that let him down. A past that would let her down too. The false sense of power, the stale pattern every one of us follows day by day, minute by minute. Excuses forwarded to the knowing section of our mind, where the knowledge of our demise sits waiting to shut down, waiting for us to turn left when we should have, oh, how we should have veered right.

Life was senseless, hope pointless, she concluded. We convince ourselves that somehow things might be different; that we will not age as he did, as she did. We won't catch the cancer that ate our neighbor's face or step lightly into traffic, too certain those amongst us are cautiously watching.

We are all going the way of the beekeeper. We—as did he—convince ourselves that death is not real, that life is not strapped for time. We ignore the certainty of it all because to face such a reality would cause us to go insane. The beekeeper, who worked his life away, leaving little time and even less love for a family who, as strange as it was, could not truly face their own life without him. He was their pillar of familiarity, and there was no room for the Reaper when the pillar stood sentry in the darkness of their farmhouse. They loathed him, then they loved him.

She straightened his tie one last time and let a smile seep from her lips. "My Papa. So handsome. As handsome as he is stubborn." She wiped a tear from her eye and released the brake on his wheelchair. "I only wanted you to be happy."

His car sat running outside the home, where so many memories whispered of ageless resentment and abandoned hopes and dreams. No longer able to drive, the beekeeper had parked the vehicle in the backfield and watched from the window as his subjects inspected its gleaming metal, hovering in wisped silence as the long grass caressed jet-black tires. She knew he loved his car, and one final ride, if nothing else, might grant her the privilege of his memory, at least long enough for him to offer her what she so desired.

Belts turning, the subtle smell of exhaust, the distant squeak of engine parts in dire need of lubrication, he felt himself lifted into the front seat, where he was met with a new awareness. The scent of leather, the potion created not by magic, but by familiarity. Like the tribe, he once held the reigns of this beast too. Long drives to the shoreline, little girl in the back seat singing with his darling...what was her name? Hot dogs at the drive-in, spilled mustard on the back seat.

"I wanted them to be happy too," he mumbled and caressed the material of his majestic creature of steel. The door slammed shut next to him, and he became aware of the stranger; she reappeared behind the steering wheel, her scent so distinguishable, crying so blatantly now.

"Don't do that," he said. He would not look in the weeper's direction; the sun too bright as it licked his cataracts, his throat too dry to raise a stiffened voice. He wanted to enjoy the ride, wanted to open the window, stick his head out and let the relentless wind blow the old age right off his bones likes candles on a birthday cake, the flames distinguished in short time.

"Papa, why won't you remember? Why don't you see me? I need you to."

In the beekeeper's mind sat a dark well. Deep in that darkness and musty in its grandeur, the open hole was where he went looking for his past. He would peer down through the blackness, holding the cool brick with trembling fingers in an instinctual attempt not to fall. Falling would surely result in death. The irony was for the old man; below him was the place all his memories had come to rest. Shelves of wooden boxes, memoirs and diaries, photographs and albums, fixtures of his life out of reach, lest he was willing to risk limbs. All he could see now, looking down with struggling eyes, was his own reflection, distorted and ageless in the stale water cradled deep down below.

The stranger wanted him to jump, the old man concluded. That was her purpose, and he read her intentions like a book. Perhaps she wanted that he lower himself by rope so that she may cut it. Her objectives were not on the up and up. He went for the door handle, tugging on the cool metal with weakened hands, but the door would not budge.

"Stop it, Papa! Please..."

"What do you want from me?" the beekeeper growled. The stranger held his arm back with one hand and steered with the other, the road before her distorted by the tears in her eyes.

"I want you to tell me you loved me. I want you to understand what you put me through over the years after Mama died. I want you to acknowledge that even after all that, I still came to you, still helped you. I've always been there for you."

He saw the stony well but was too stubborn to approach. He would go there in his own time. He was master of so many, humming in swarms, crawling on skin, stinging and dying, all the while he held his command of them as they provided their Majesty with liquid gold, day after day.

"I want you to remember. Remember the picture frame I made you on Father's day, how I put in a photograph of myself and wrapped it in foil and red ribbon. I left it on the table for you so that you might find it before breakfast. You didn't even open it, Papa! *You never even opened it!*"

He turned his face from her and glanced past the well. They drove past fields where the hives once lay, monumental of his success. At one time, they were full of life; the buzzing could be heard from the house at times so perfect, it played tricks on the stranger's young ears. She would stop and listen as the steady scream lifted and dropped from her left ear to her right, a seesaw of audio that caused a vibration on the back of her tongue. The hives were gone now, along with her father's tribe of dancing wings. Their master now a skeleton of what once was sat next to her quietly pouting. He would go to the well when he was ready.

"I just wanted some answers. Mama wanted them too—I know she did. She wanted to know how you could be so cold to us, Papa—pretend like we were not even there at times. We were good to you, Papa. I was a good girl, wasn't I?" She sobbed and turned the steering wheel. The beekeeper felt the blood in his head adjust as the car ascended a distantly familiar hill. He stared at his hands and wondered whose they were—so sickly, so bony under stretched spotty skin. They surely were no longer his own.

The stranger parked the car, and a silence descended as the motor rocked ever so gently. She turned to him. "Look at me," she said. With a tender hand, she turned the old man's face towards her. "See me, Papa?" His eyes would not roll. She wiped a tear from her own. Outside, willow trees swayed in the gentle wind. "See me. Please!"

She waited for him to come back to her, waited for that moment when his eyes readjusted to his life, and everything came back into perspective. There would be a spark, a glimpse of love, enough to carry her through the rest of her days, as short as they might be.

When there was nothing, she dropped her hand from his chin, and the beekeeper's gaze fell back on his lap. "I'm dying, Papa. I have cancer. I can't take care of you anymore. I don't have the energy, and I don't have much time. That's why I brought you here."

The stranger got out of the car and closed the door, leaving him alone with his thoughts. He looked back to the well in his mind and shook his head. A sudden gust of air and hum, and his door opened. She lifted his gaunt body out of the car and into his wheelchair, adjusting his slipper-covered feet so they would not drag along the ground. Through his tainted eyes, the beekeeper made out monuments. Alone and cold, each one spread across fields like hives. Statues of angels, broken noses, and chipped grey cheeks looked back at him. She pushed him towards a fresh grave; the soil, black and pure as her intentions, as fresh as youth was its scent. Dead flowers consumed his vision, and he attempted in vain to read the epitaph.

She put the break on his wheelchair, and he waited in silence while she prayed. When she was finished, she leaned down to him.

"I wanted you to see Mama one last time."

Wind whispered of finality. Grass, crisp and yellow, twirled slightly amidst fallen leaves and twigs. In the distance, the hum was steady.

The stranger had to fight to get Mother buried where she now rested. The cemetery was no longer cared for. Grass no longer mowed, weeds no longer pulled—but it was where Mama wanted them to be. Next to her grave was the old man's. Born in 1929, it read. Waiting patiently sat his

The Beekeeper

granite marking, a single bee etched onto its reflective surface, the ground still unbroken. It would not be long.

She wheeled him further up the hill then, kicking stones from under the chair's rubber tires. Struggling with each step, she sometimes turned and dragged him as the summoning hum grew louder. In the center of the cemetery stood a small chapel. Wilting roof, and windows broken by rock wielding children, it stood humble. White paint on walls struggling to stay longer, just as the beekeeper was. In this place, one could still find solace, but to enter now was simply taboo...unless you were him.

She stopped in front of the chapel and kneeled down again. "I will walk you to the front door, Papa. From there, you go inside yourself. I love you." She left a kiss on his cheek, and for a moment, he cherished the warmth of her lips. She raised him out of his chair and placed his wooden cane in his left hand. He gripped it awkwardly. Finally finding a comfortable position, he slid one foot in front of the other, her arms entangled in his. The humming was comforting, beckoning, and his mind eased.

At the front of the chapel, a tiny latch was all that held the door closed; the sweet scent of honey overwhelming. The door creaked open with an easy push, and the distant hum became thunder. The old man gasped as she let go of his arm and backed away from the overwhelming sight. Through the swarm he walked, his hand holding his body rigid, and he slid himself gracefully along the wall, all his weight countered only by his cane. He disappeared into the shadows, and the door closed behind him.

At the side of the chapel, one single window was still intact. The stranger pushed her nose up against the pane and watched the old man find a place to sit at the front pew. He leaned his cane against its fine wood and smiled as the swarm surrounded him. The walls of the chapel now formed of honeycomb, liquid gold ran in streams of glisten, and he smiled and looked around slowly. He was with his subjects, and they were with the beekeeper as one, together in the hive. He would not die alone, as his wife had done, as his Molly would do soon. She began to cry again as Papa grimaced in pain, each stinger finding a soft spot upon his skin. Spectacular streams of yellow and black painted his clothing and danced upon his flesh. He put his arms out in a welcoming gesture.

Bodies of bees lay in heaps around the old man's slippers. Each one took turns stinging, an organized ritual of passing. And with every sting, the beekeeper's mind relaxed, and he went to the well he so adamantly avoided and saw that his memories floated in the rising water. He relaxed his fingers and lips as the venom of the bees entered his bloodstream and became sedative, releasing his once-imprisoned mind.

The water continued to rise, and he realized his belongings, his memories were within reach. The golden retriever and the litter of puppies ran beside him. The red kite he lost in the oak tree as a child. His mother, and her splendid, simple beauty. Arms out, they embraced, and he cried, tears streaming down silly, grinning cheeks. The scent of the honey in his nostrils so overwhelming. He opened his eyes and drifted—his body became lighter, and he turned to the window, where the sobbing stranger watched. She saw the glimmer in his eye…

"Molly," he said and smiled. His eyes opened and closed; the sting of each bee became a gentle nudge into the afterworld. "My Molly… How I am sorry. How I loved you, little girl…"

It was enough. Molly put her fingers to the windowpane and watched the old man close his eyes one last time. The bees took him as one of their own, a gesture of love left and compassion saved for but a few. She was satisfied, as the lump in her throat suggested. She would leave him there to be with them, a tomb, a hive, a just ending for a man so distant from her, yet still forever residing, always in her heart. She would face her own fate alone, just as the rest of us often do, but she would face it knowing the beekeeper loved her all the same.

Biography

James Cheetham is a dark fiction writer from Manitoba, Canada. He lives with his wife Tanya and young daughter Stephanie.

To read more about James Cheetham, visit his blog:

www.fadetopalemanuscript.blogspot.com

The Country Faire
by
Marva Dasef

 At the first annual Country Faire in 1973, I joined my group from University to sell ice cream to raise funds. Fifteen women took turns at the booth, enjoying the hot summer days. Days that wore on languidly with a hot sun hanging heavy; my shoulders burned from its ferocity. Customers chatted animatedly, their voices combining with the sounds of laughter, bird calls, and buzzing bees. The ice cream we decided to sell turned out to be a good choice, and I partook of one or two myself. Its coldness was a balm on my tongue and dry throat.

 I volunteered to be an overnighter. Since the booth was open air, we needed someone in it twenty-four hours a day to protect our investment. A lot of people camped with tents or just slept out under the stars. Camping didn't faze me. After all, I'd participated in such events every year of my youth—Mom and Dad insisted on dragging us to local beauty spots and setting up camp for the weekend. Frugal living, but, looking back, I'd say they were the best times of my life.

 That night, drums beat loudly. Vendors partied around a cozy bonfire. Their bonhomie lured me to join them. The acrid stench of smoke assailed my nostrils and made my eyes water as I drew closer to the fire. I sat and watched them for a while under the clear diamond-lit night, joining in with their songs and light-hearted banter. An hour later, the temperature dropped. A chilly breeze nipped at my skin. Goose bumps stood proudly, and I rubbed the tops of my arms in an effort to banish them. I yawned and my eyelids drooped. Saying my farewells, I returned to the tent-booth and snuggled in my warm down-filled sleeping bag.

 An urge to pee woke me. Darkness engulfed the tent. My distended bladder throbbed, hurt. I hauled myself out of my snug sleeping bag and shuffled on hands and knees to the tent opening. My period had started, and the pressure on my bladder sent painful cramps through my abdomen and down into my thighs. I rummaged around for the flashlight, then trudged off into the trees to the row of porta-johns. Night moisture graced the grass, and the trees loomed before me like verdant men; branches jutted out—wooden arms, gnarled knuckles and all. A shiver beset my spine and, shrugging off my unease, I tugged at the metal handle on the first porta-john in the line and breathed a sigh of relief to find it unoccupied.

 Not wanting to sit on what I couldn't see, I crouched over the hole and balanced my torch on the edge of the seat. The ammonia smell of stale urine assailed my nostrils and my eyes watered. My throat constricting, I held back a gag, slapped my palm over my mouth and swallowed. I tried to go about my task as fast as I could. My butt nudged the torch. Its beam wavered and dimmed.

Damn batteries...

A rustle outside. Someone walking past the john? Footsteps squished in the mud outside the door, then stopped. My heart thudded and joined in with the steady pace of the footsteps. They stopped. I held my breath. The door ripped open and crashed against the side of the porta-john. A muscular arm hurled my flashlight into the woods before I could see his face. I let out the breath I'd held along with a terrified squeal. A black figure, against a dark night, loomed in the doorway. Bulky. Big.

He stepped forward and shoved me back on the hard seat. Pain shot from my hips and clawed up my spine. Heart hammering, my gaze flicked around the john. Escape? Impossible. The man slammed his hand over my mouth and yanked me standing. I struggled to open my mouth in an attempt to scream; my tongue came into contact with his palm, tasted beer and smoke. Striking out with my arms and legs, I tried to wrestle him from me, but was trapped in the foul box allowing no escape.

"Don't make a sound or you're dead." His voice, a fear-inspiring rasp, rumbled around the john. Nausea grew and lodged itself in the form of a lump in my throat.

Please don't hurt me... Please, just let me go...

He moved his thumb over my nostrils and pressed my head into the backboard. I couldn't breathe, much less scream. The unmistakable whisper of a zipper... My eyes widened, ached. Lungs bursting for air, I brought my hands up to his wrist and tried to pull his hand away. He pressed harder. I longed to scream; widened my eyes further, trying to get a glimpse of his face. So dark, I saw nothing but an outline against the tiny screened window of the porta-john.

He moved his thumb, and I inhaled that much longed for oxygen. Realization dawned. I quit struggling, wanting it to be over. Sweat rolled down my face, and the lump in my throat grew bigger, threatening to choke me. He entered me easily; I was almost thankful for that. He thrust forward and back... Grunted like a pig. My body stayed rigid with fear, my mind retreating to a faraway place where the sun shone, daisies danced in the cool breeze, a stream trickled nearby.

Finally, he pulled his body away. One hand still clamped to my mouth, he brought his other between us. A cold, sharp blade pressed against my neck.

"Lay down on the floor."

I complied.

Please don't let him cut me...

He pressed the blade and sliced. I felt my skin opening like a Ziploc bag, brought my hand up to the wound on instinct. He snatched his hand from my mouth and quickly exited the tiny box, leaving me to struggle back up into a sitting position. Blood trickled between my fingers and down my neck to my chest.

Should I scream now? Will screaming make the blood flow faster? My carotid artery must be intact—I'm alive. What if he comes back to finish the job?

I listened. Complete silence except for the call of an owl and the faint thrum of the drums beating in tempo with my heart. The man was long gone.

I bunched my shirt up against the wound with trembling hands. Standing, dizziness hit me, the burning flames of Hell speeding through my nerve endings. Panic caused my heart to beat faster, to throb so violently, I imagined it bursting out of my chest.

I looked out of the doorway. Pre-dawn light tinged the trees, lit those verdant men so that I fancied I saw grotesque faces with leering smiles. Shifting my gaze to the faint outlines of the tents, I pulled myself together as best I could and made my way back to the booth. Hollow, hollow inside, it seemed my body was now void, contained no innards. Tears trickled down my cheeks. Still holding my shirt against my neck, I crawled back into my tent.

Should I wake the others? What would they do? Sympathize? Certainly, but not much more. I haven't seen the face of my assailant. Out of the hundreds of people who are camping at the Faire, there would be no way to find him...

I exchanged my bunched shirt for a cloth, pressed it against my neck until dawn pinked the eastern sky. Mind numb, I woke the others.

"What the hell...?"

"Where did that blood come from? Are you all right?"

"You need to go to hospital. I'll call an ambulance."

I'm not hurt too badly on the outside. No, not on the outside...

At least, the cut on my neck didn't hurt and ache as much as the rest of my bruised body.

At the hospital, the nurse took a rape sample. The police said there was little chance of finding the rapist. He could have been anyone...

They dropped the case of the Faire rape of 1973 for lack of any clues.

The County Faire

I'm lucky he didn't kill me, I know that. But my dreams—or I should say nightmares—are suffused with the smell of feces and urine in an outhouse. I see the port-a-john in my dreams and, unlike the reality, excrement has been smeared on the walls and toilet seat. Urine puddles decorate the floor, morph into a river of fear. And he enters my nighttime movie, face unseen, his face black, as if hidden by a mask. I suffer the rape in my nightmares night after night after night.

Regardless, life goes on. I continue to make my yearly trek to the Country Faire. Seldom do I find the right height and weight, but some men have the same fetid odor. At times, I just get the right *feeling* about someone—a little tingle in my belly or a quick flash of adrenaline speeding my pulse when I notice a hulking figure. Even then, I'm not always lucky enough that he goes to the porta-johns in the middle of the night.

Still, I'm patient. When it does come together perfectly, I follow him. The screwdriver I carry makes it easy to break the weak lock. Most often, he is facing the wall and does not see the blade that I draw across his neck in one swift and satisfying slice.

The Hunter
by
Marva Dasef

He glanced up and down the dark street and saw no one. Shrugging the overcoat's collar higher up his neck, he slipped into the shadowed alleyway. Once hidden from prying eyes, he took the mask from his pocket and put it on, adjusting it to ensure that he could see without interference. He leaned back against the rough brick wall. And waited.

His thoughts wandered to the delights he would soon partake. The wide-eyed fear, the mouth gaping open to scream just as he crushed the lips against the teeth. Blood flowing between his fingers would be a pleasing touch. He mused about some kind of wrapping with sharp edges for his hands, perhaps gloves with barbed wire. Embedded glass would be too difficult to attach.

The sharp rap of high heels broke his reverie, and he pressed closer to the shadowed wall.

Yes, tight skirt practically exposing her buttocks, low-cut blouse plunging down to her artificially enhanced cleavage. Open-toed shoes. Just what he wanted. And, so soon. A bonus.

He stepped forward, and with practiced ease wrapped his arm around her neck and pushed his palm against the bright red lips. The struggle was good. She writhed, and he heard her rasping in an attempt to breathe around his hand; three fingers across the mouth with thumb and forefinger pinching her nostrils shut. He'd worked long and hard to make this move work every time. The effort paid off; her heaving body slumped against his.

Closed his eyes and shuddered. Too soon, too soon. Gritting his teeth to slow his pounding pulse and quiet his lust, he dragged the near limp body deeper into the dark alley. Holding still, he waited for the chest to quit heaving, seeking air. He laid the body down almost tenderly and drew the scalpel from its hiding place. Slipping its edge under the top button of her blouse, with a twitch of his wrist, the button flew away into the darkness.

Work slowly... No need to rush. Savor every moment...

He sighed. It took so little time these days; he'd become too practiced at his art.

Maybe something different? Should I start at the bottom, just for variety's sake?

Kneeling beside her, his gaze roamed down her legs to her feet. Smooth. White. Red toenails. Perfect. He lifted the edge of the short skirt, exposing lacy red panties.

Crotchless. How crude.

Using the scalpel with finesse, he sliced open the skirt and the panties. His gaze fell on her shaved pubes, and he imagined her dressed in a schoolgirl's outfit.

Plaid skirt and a white blouse.

He sighed again and pressed the scalpel down just above her slit. He started to cut upwards on her soft belly.

An arm wrapped around his neck and snapped his head backwards. Twisting to look down at the whore's face, he couldn't quite make it out. She was no longer lying flat on the ground, but sitting up with a strong forearm against his throat.

He dropped the scalpel and tried to raise his hands, hoping that would be enough for her to let him go, to run away. Instead, she pulled him up, and his feet no longer touched the filthy cement of the alley. Held up by his neck, he gasped trying to draw air into his lungs. The grip on his neck was too tight; lack of air turned his vision red and he felt his eyes bulge. The last thing he heard was a howl close by his ear. A howl that would turn blood cold. A howl calling a pack to fresh meat.

Coward
by
Marva Dasef

Gina pulled her legs tighter to her chest and covered her head with her arms. The heavy boot would aim for her stomach this time—she just knew it. The blow did not come. She opened one eye and saw the foot a few inches from her head. The master stood with hands on knees gasping for breath. Maybe he had finished with her for now.

Reaching out, she touched the toe of his boot. "Master, please, kick me again."

He pulled away from her hand. With a snort of disgust, the master turned away and walked out of the room.

Gina didn't move for a few minutes; assessed the damage. The pain began to fade and she slowly straightened her legs. She pushed on her rib cage with tentative fingers, pressing harder in her search for broken bones. This time, there were none. The bruises would last for days, she knew. The sound of sobs bounced off the walls. The new girl tied in the corner. Gina didn't bother trying to soothe her. It would do no good.

She rolled to her belly and pushed herself up with aching arms. Not too bad, she thought. If she could placate the master long enough for the bruises to heal, she'd live another week, a month, maybe months. But she was in no doubt about what would finally happen. She'd seen the bodies dragged out to the back, glimpsed the mounded earth, a scraggly shrub planted to hide the freshly turned soil.

Was it two months now? Remembering the passing days proved difficult. She slept when she could, blocked all memory of what had passed and all realization of what was to come. Her life ended the day her father accepted the master's bag of coins. Nothing afterwards counted, not when you're already dead inside.

Why did she try to keep breathing? Some primordial instinct, the self-survival her brain demanded? She'd learned her lesson the first week. The master forced her to watch while he tortured two other girls to death. They'd cried in pain and begged him to stop. He'd turned to her where she lay trussed in the corner.

"See, see. They're afraid. That's their mistake. If they asked for more, then I'd stop. I only hit them because they are cowards. I hate cowards."

Gina understood his need to hear his victims cry out their agony, beg for mercy. Once she'd seen a girl die in a pool of blood, she resolved to be different. He still beat and kicked her, but stopped short of the fatal

The Hunter

blow when she continued to ask for more. She promised herself she would survive this. Playing his game.

At some point, she realized that *she* was the coward. Afraid to die, she asked for more. Her stomach turned at how she lacked courage. Yes, *she* was the coward. Gina wished she could be brave...and die.

Heather's Pain
by
Marva Dasef

Heather woke up every morning for the last week well before dawn. She couldn't get to sleep, stayed awake almost until morning, only to have her racing mind kick her into wakefulness after too few hours of sleep.

Her doctor prescribed a new medication, but she didn't think it was working very well. Hers was a pain a chemical could not easily mask. Dr. Montoya said it might take time for the drug to take effect. She was way past the point of narcotic drugs helping.

I'll call the doctor today for an appointment. There has to be something else he can do.

She scrunched to one side, putting her legs over the edge of the bed, allowing gravity to draw her legs to the floor as she performed a slow motion roll. Once she was kneeling by the side of the bed, she pushed herself up, wincing from the pain in her back. She ached all over, but her back was the center. Jetting pain shot down from her hips to her ankles.

Sciatica. And I'm only thirty.

She shuffled to the bathroom. Grabbing the handicap bar she had installed, she slowly lowered herself onto the toilet. Finishing, she pulled herself up with the bar and tottered to the sink.

To keep from falling, she stood straight upright as she brushed her teeth. Barely tipping her head forward, she managed to spit the toothpaste into the sink rather than down her front. Sick to death of this pain; yes, she'd see the doctor and tell him she must have the surgery, despite the risks. She could not continue to live like this. The constriction on her spine had grown steadily, the pain getting worse. Osteoporosis coupled with stenosis. It sounded almost lyrical, but the pain felt far from poetic. She had no reason to wait any longer.

Pushing her feet into her slippers, she held the door jamb for support, glad she didn't have to spend another day in her nightgown. Her mom was coming over this morning to help her out. Maybe then she could get dressed.

For now, all she could do was lower herself stiffly onto the lounge chair. She picked up the remote, turned on the TV, and flipped through channels. Nothing held her attention for long, but it helped to pass the time. Reading was impossible; she couldn't concentrate. Even something light like a Harlequin Romance required more thought than she could muster.

She wished she had a cup of coffee, but didn't have the energy to fight to get herself up and shuffle to the kitchen.

I'll wait until mom gets here.

Heather dozed for a while, only to wake at the same time the back door slammed.

"Mom?" she called out, but got no answer. Again, "Is that you, Mom?"

Maybe I shouldn't have left the door unlocked for Mother. I should have given her a key. Why didn't I think of that?

She sat and waited, hoped her mom had simply not heard her call out. Maybe she was putting up groceries in the kitchen. Was the kitchen out of earshot? She stared at the entrance to the living room from where she sat in her chair. The hallway led to the kitchen with a swinging door she usually left propped open, but it could have swung shut. That was it. Her mom was in the kitchen putting away food and didn't hear her call. She'd just wait and soon her mother would come down the hall.

Footsteps sounded in the hallway.

"Mom?" she called again.

A man, short and close to being fat, appeared in the doorway. Dressed in a dark blue hooded sweatshirt, with the hood up. Heather absurdly noticed his muscular chest and that he'd covered his face with something. A black ski mask? The man hesitated for a moment, as if surprised to see her.

Heather opened her mouth to scream, but he was across the room much faster than she thought possible. He jammed his hand against her mouth, stifling the scream before it could get started.

"Shut your mouth, bitch, or I'll kill you."

She looked into his eyes and knew he wasn't lying; nodded her head slightly to show she understood. Slowly, he drew his hand away from her mouth.

He glanced around the room, probably looking for anything valuable to haul off. His gaze fell on the side table by her chair, where she kept her array of daytime meds. He grabbed them up, reading the labels. He shoved the bottle of oxycontin into his pocket and swept the rest onto the floor.

"You're sick, eh?" he said while prowling the room picking up objects and discarding them as worthless. "What's amatter?"

"My back," she said. "I've got a bad back."

He jerked her to her feet. She screamed in pain and collapsed to the floor.

"Get up," he said roughly.

"I can't!" she sobbed.

"Well, that's a good thing," he chuckled, "for me." He looked around and saw the door leading to her bedroom. She left it ajar as she always did. He went into the bedroom and she heard him rummaging through her things; the sound of glass breaking, a heavy thump as something hit the floor.

Sudden anger overrode her fear; the feeling of violation she'd heard described by people who were robbed. It drove her mad she was so helpless. All she could do was listen as her cherished things crashed to the floor.

She couldn't take it anymore. Gritting her teeth, she grasped the arms of the chair and pushed herself up from the floor. Staggering to the fireplace, she grabbed the poker and moved quietly to her bedroom door, standing to one side of it, hidden from view. She raised the poker over her shoulder and tightened her muscles in anticipation. As the thief came out, she smashed his face with the poker. He dropped to the floor, no sound coming from his mouth. Raising the poker, she hit him again. And, again. Anger overwhelmed her, and she struck the man's head until it was a bloody mess.

Heather stood panting over the lifeless body. *Oh, my God…What have I done? I should have hit him only once. Now they'll arrest me, put me in jail. At the very least, the police will question me. They won't care if I have a bad back or not, whether he'd robbed me or not…*

Was this self-defense? She didn't know, but was afraid to find out.

The back door opened and closed again. Her mother called out, "It's me, dear. Shall I make you a cup of tea?" before walking into the living room. She stared at the body lying on the floor and her daughter still holding the poker. Her mouth opened and closed in an attempt to speak.

"What happened? Who is that?" she finally gasped out.

Calm now, Heather told her what happened. Her mother took all of this in, then said, "We'll bury the body. Nobody will think to look around here for him." Heather breathed out in relief. Her mother, what would she do without her?

Between them, they dragged the dead thief out to the backyard. The high fence and shrubbery hid the yard from possible prying eyes. In the far back corner, Heather had started a compost heap. No longer used as she couldn't take care of a garden, it stood heaped high with dead leaves and grass clippings.

The two women looked at the compost heap, then at each other. Heather found two shovels in the shed, handed one to her mother without a word, and they began to dig. The compost had been warmed by the sun, yet still held dew enabling them to dig down through it easily.

Too bad. This stuff would be really good for the garden…

As they dug, she realized her back didn't hurt. This turn of events surprised her. The violent actions had loosened the grip of her spine on frayed nerves. She would be better, at least for a while. This thought made

Heather's Pain

her grimly happy.
Two birds with one poker.
She started to cry as her mother embraced her.
Tears streaming down her face, she loosed herself from her mother's grasp and bent down to toss the last handful of dirt on the compost pile.

Biography

Marva Dasef is a writer living in Oregon. Retired from thirty-five years in the software industry, she has now turned her energies to writing fiction, a much more satisfying occupation. She lives with her husband, Jack, and two lazy cats (don't all writers?). Marva graduated from the University of Oregon far back in the mists of time. She has two grown sons who, thankfully, have not yet boomeranged back home. She has published more than thirty stories in a variety of print and online journals. See all her published works on her website: http://www.marvadasef.com/.

The Game
by
M.E Ellis
(Previously published on Demon Minds)

There is a Rubik's cube in my head. For everything to fall into place, the side that faces me must all be one colour. As each requirement is filled, so is another square. I have one square to fill for the last side to be complete. For the whole cube to be finished.

Sally was white, the first—my actions bright and fresh, pure. Laura was blue, the penultimate; the colour denoting my sadness that this fun is coming to an end. Those in between, pah! Forget them, I have. And you, you are red, for the danger. That my luck could be running out. Surely, it must. A chance I have to take, for I long to have you.

Short, spiky brown hair. I wonder if the words from your tongue will be as sharp? That envy of my excellence may flow from your eyes to match their greenness. Is your skin really as delicious as fresh cream? We shall see.

Yes. Indeed. We. Will.

You are here. Can you see yourself on my map—that big red arrow pointing to your position? You step towards my car, get in the passenger seat. Strap yourself in. I slide into gear, pull away from the kerb and turn off my FOR HIRE light. The last red square is nearly filled. My cube will be complete. Everything will have fallen into place.

We slide through the slick streets, rain drizzling, slithering down the windshield. You glance and see there is no fare metre, no radio handset. Pat your handbag absently, glancing out of the window to your left, hoping, *hoping* I am not the one you were warned about. Not *him*.

But. I. Am.

Nervous now, aren't you? I take a right turn, you take a sidelong look at my profile, just in case you escape. It will do you no good. If you had looked at me when you got in the car you would have seen that I had a black leather mask on. Too late. You're locked in. With me.

Gloves, yes, leather gloves, squeaking their newness against the steering wheel. Fresh pair each time. Over the engine I almost persuade myself I can hear your heart thrumming frantically against your ribcage. Scary... isn't it?

The rutted track causes the car to jostle on its axles, groan in protest at the uneven ground. I reverse into a siding, point the car back the way we came, stop the engine.

Your eyes move from side to side, chest rising in panic, hands gripping your bag handle. White knuckles. Lips quivering, longing to stretch wide in a gurn, while your tears spill free.

"What is your name?"

That darting look again.

"Cheryl." Small, unsure smile. Downcast lashes; damp.

"I'm Rob. Pleased to meet you. From now on you will respond to the name Red. Clear?"

Frown. A whispered yes.

"A little stuffy in here, don't you think, Red? It's time we got started. Get that rucksack from the foot well and open it. Put the mask on."

Nod. Tiny nod. Reduced to feeling five-years-old, just like that. Reaching for the bag, unzipping it with trembling fingers, you look inside and bring out the mask. Your face registers concern of mammoth proportions. Yes, you know for definite it is me. I am *him*.

"I'll just let you out, and we can begin."

I reach for my dart gun, get out of the car, leave my door open, and stroll to yours.

"Out! Leave the rucksack. You can take your bag."

You do as you are told. Good girl.

"Now run! Run!"

You dither, not knowing what to do. Should you run? I would, if I were you.

"*RUN!*"

And you do, across the field, keeping to the hedges, mask against your face, deer antlers bobbing.

"Gallop!" I shout, "Like a gazelle! Graceful!"

And you do.

I give chase, gun in hand, ready to strike you down should your pace slacken, your stride falter, your lack of breath cause you to stop. Through the woods we go, the hunter and the hunted, crashing through bushes, undergrowth threatening to trip us at every turn.

"Careful with those steps you take, Red! I'm right behind you! Run! Run for your life!" I cackle, a maniacal burst of mirth unlike any other I have experienced before. You're heading for the motorway to safety. Clever girl.

I speed up, but in the other direction, back to where I came from, wanting to get you just when you think you are free, just as you flag down a car…just when your heart begins to slow with relief.

I am at my car, FOR HIRE sign removed, in, belted, driving, racing at speed to where you will emerge. Slowing down, parking on the verge.

The Game

Watching, waiting.

Through the last thicket of trees and you're out. Onto the motorway, hands flailing in the air, a macabre sight in your head gear, a human moose, running full pelt towards oncoming traffic that swerves to avoid such an insane sight. A drunk out on a dare, someone to be avoided despite the news coverage of women being shot with animal darts—elephant, rhino, and zebra masks adorning their heads. They have forgotten all ready.

I pull up beside you, and in panic you jump in.

"Get me out of here, please...please!" you say, pulling off the mask, tears spilling, red cheeks stained by black mascara. Turning, turning to me as you hear the door locks click, eyes wide as I say,

"Sure, Red."

Serenity Sea
by
M.E Ellis

Brain pulled through your nostrils with a hook. Empty head, empty head. Eye sockets devoid of eyeballs, removed by my gouging fingers, the resulting cavities seemingly fathoms deep. Tongue sawn away, a stump at the back of your throat—no more admonishments—my ears in bliss at the hum silence creates. Your cheeks carved as a pumpkin, the tea light sits inside your mouth to illuminate my creation. Left—the devil you were in life. Right—the angel I wish you had been.

Times past, the yen for your acceptance burned so fiercely I fancied I tasted the resulting ash, for all fires are doused eventually. I accepted defeat, acted on impulse to rid my life of the pain you were.

Fires. One small spark grows to inferno proportions before petering out. I'm petering out now, my zest for retribution assuaged. Peace runs through my veins, replacing the blood of the unhappy. Calmness pervades my soul—the itch of irritation scratched away. Floating on Serenity Sea, tranquillity overrides previous ills, and my lips tug upwards. Big smile, big smile.

Aren't you just pretty? No venom spewing from your mouth, no brain to form the ever-growing list of orders. No *you*. One time irks me beyond others, one time out of so many...

"Peter?"

"Yes, ma'am?"

"I want to eat."

"I don't want to feed you, ma'am."

"Do it."

You doused my innocent fire. The sizzle of the tea light causes tears to pinch my eyes. A bliss encompasses my whole being. I have filled your mouth with the very thing you always ordered from the menu. It protrudes from your lips, an obscene sight. You were *always* hungry. I no longer want that tainted thing to be a part of me. Yours forever.

The Stanza
by
M.E Ellis

Shorn of head, wide of girth,
Face of fun, full of mirth.

My mission: to find someone of that description and quite simply, kill them.

I see my target while sitting in the snug of a pub. This is hardly my choice of establishment, but I spotted her as she legged it down the street at the highest speed her body would carry her. Following her into this rundown place—that only the locals would want to frequent—I settle myself down to watch.

I squint across at the bar and exhale smoke from my lungs through barely open lips. Spot her. She is jovial, overly so, with the required shorn head and wide hips. I lean back on the leather sofa and continue to smoke and stare. She sees me, of course she does, but she pretends she has not. No matter, she will be mine tonight.

The volume of voices becomes raucous as more alcohol is consumed. I've nursed the same pint since I sat down. She walks over to my table. I do not expect confrontation; the gaze I direct upon her is hopefully seductive.

"Hey, babe!" I cringe at her familiarity. They say it breeds contempt. The thirst for my reason increases. My pulse quickens, and blood rises to the surface of my cheeks.

"Shy?" she quips with the tone of one who is used to telling jokes and being laughed with. She is confident. This may be a slight hindrance but nothing I have not handled before.

"A little." I glance up through lowered lids.

"You want another pint, babe?" Her fleshy lips break into a beam, revealing thick pale gums. Her jagged teeth, yellow with brown stains from smoking. Unappealing.

"Please." Passing her my glass, our fingers touch. Hers feel rough and worn as if she uses bleach to wash them.

She walks to the bar, and I watch her order. She glances my way, sees I am watching and gives me a coy smile. I suspect she didn't think she would *score* so easily. How I hate that term.

I marvel, as I always do, at the fact that I know the moments they now spend with me are their last. That they do not know what is coming, do not have the choice to act accordingly as they would if they had been given the nod that this was their time. A smile tugs at the corners of my mouth, and I stifle the urge to laugh out loud.

She walks back over to my table. Sits beside me, hand upon my thigh. I shudder inwardly, control my instinct to recoil.

"What's your name, doll?" Her hand massages my leg.

"Charlotte."

"Nice. Mine's whatever you want to call me." She throws back her head at her own joke. Silver fillings in all of her top teeth. She does not take care of herself. Her body size denotes her menu, skin indicates her choice of liquid. Broken veins grace her nose and cheeks, raised red pimples reside on her chin. She is, without a doubt, quite revolting.

"I'll call you Pamela." My eyelids flutter and I cast my gaze down to the tabletop.

"I look like a Pam, huh? Cool." She smiles. Her grin turns my stomach. "Well, Charlotte. Shall we leave this place and go to mine after this drink?" Her fingers still rub the fabric of my trousers, setting my teeth on edge.

"If you like."

"Oh, darling. I *do* like."

She winks.

* * *

I sleep with her. Body flaccid and clammy. All in the cause. Her thighs squeeze mine as we writhe on her futon. She produces sweat like a man on a workout and repulses me beyond measure.

We shower and drink tea. She falls asleep sitting up. I stroke her hair, and her mouth gapes. She snores. Spit oozes from the corner of her lips, pools onto her heaving chest where her chin rests.

I wash up the cups, use her rubber gloves. Wipe everything I've touched. I dress, stand, and watch her for a while.

I imagine her with hair the colour of chestnuts, rich and full of lustre. Not the shorn off crop she actually has. She does look like a Pamela I once knew. As they all did, in some way or another. The rage within has been building steadily all night, and soon it will reach the peak that ensures I will do the task.

I pace. Clutch at my hair, see the terrible visions that blight my existence. The real Pam smirking at me before she slaps… Pam coming at me with a wooden spoon ready to wield it upon my flesh… Yanking my hair back as I try to run away.

The Stanza

She ended up running when I turned on her with a carving knife. I've never seen her since. Except in my mind.

Memories spiral. Kaleidoscopic images merge and blur. Rage burns within, brings acid and bile into my throat, causes me to choke. I swallow it back.

The rubber gloves make my hands sweat, their small size tight against my fingers. I look at the form on the futon. Lolling head, mouth agape. The tide is too strong to hold back.

Wide of girth, foul of face,
This Pam takes the old Pam's place.

Her face resembles a colander. Slits and holes. The skin on her hands like ripped leather gloves from her pathetic attempts to protect herself. Her throat, a shark's sneer, fat globules as its teeth. Her chest a fisherman's net; my blade swiped to and fro across it.

She is, of course, quite dead, this Pam.

I leave her home, wear the gloves as far as the corner grocery shop near her flat. I place them under a full black refuse sack.

Pamela. Pam. Mother.

I pick up my book of poems.

Long of hair, slender of build,
Bosoms a plenty, milk they yield,
Child of her womb, carried in arms,
Freckles on nose, a part of her charms.

Maurice's Job
by
M.E Ellis

Maurice liked to deliver flowers to the funeral of everyone he helped on the journey to Heaven. He chose each set of blooms specifically for that person. Roses for the blonde girl with the pink cheeks. Lilies delivered graveside for the pale-skinned brunette. Violets for the redhead—matched the purple bruises.

He stood and watched the funeral cortege make its way up the winding path. Shielded under the eaves of the church doorway, Maurice witnessed the tearful mourners gagging on their own spittle. Hitching breaths his Prozac—each ragged gasp his medicine.

He sat on the back pew and listened to the priest lament the terrible waste of life. Smiled tightly and cocked his head to the side to better hear the stifled sobs, the rustle of scrunched up tissues. Black hats bobbed in sorrow. Maurice showed his uneven teeth, lips drawn back—blanched of colour.

Butterflies flitted within. Mirth threatened to spew, yearned to echo in the rafters. He anchored the unruly urges. It wouldn't do to laugh. Instead, he inhaled deeply. Bibles, years old, yielded their musty scent. Maurice enjoyed the smell of death.

* * *

Reckless, walking home alone. Maurice watched her saunter, hips swaying from too much alcohol. He wondered if she felt light-headed as she weaved along the path.

Pursuing at a quiet pace, Maurice stalked his prey. His soft-soled shoes ensured his secrecy—his tread unnoticed in the night's stillness.

Her stilettos tapped the pavement, the sound echoing, giving the illusion of many women walking. He sneered to himself and crept on, his palms sweaty. Heart aflutter, he quelled the laughter that tapped at his lips. The time to giggle could wait.

Swathed in a black overcoat, leather gloves of the same hue, he shortened the gap between himself and the woman. She turned the corner into a darkened alley. Maurice upped his pace.

Lit at each end by the orange glow of streetlamps, darkness shrouded the alley's centre. Her silhouette meandered from side to side. Maurice's soles slapped against the rain-slicked concrete. She didn't hear him until he was upon her, his palm clamped over her mouth. Her knees buckled, and the stench of warm urine assaulted him.

His deed done, her heart no longer beating its frightened tattoo, he thought of the flowers he would bring to her grave.

* * *

"Hello again, sir! What would you like today?"

Maurice closed the florist shop door. The bell above it tinkled a cheery tone. The smell of flora assailed him, and he took a deep breath. Holding the air in his lungs for two seconds, he released it through pursed lips.

He adjusted his black-framed glasses and plastered on a smile, clasped his hands together over his distended stomach. Maurice flicked out his tongue to wet his lips, replied, "I'd like a large bouquet of daffodils, please!"

Yellow daffodils, the colour of her liquid emission.

Rocking on his heels, he twiddled his fingers against the backs of his putty coloured hands and surveyed the florist's ample behind. His grey suit trousers felt uncomfortably tight. The fabric tented beneath his zipper. He cleared his throat. His heart quickened at the sight of the woman's shapely calves.

"Your wife is a lucky woman, sir. I wish my husband would buy me flowers every week!" The florist's voice sounded muffled as she bent over a large bucket containing the yellow spring bells.

Maurice chuckled. "Yes, well. We can't all be of the same mould now can we? Life would be boring if we all did similar things."

If people did similar things to me, the population would decrease dramatically!

Maurice stifled a giggle.

* * *

The hearse crawled down Main Street. Elderly people doffed their hats and lowered heads to chests. Middle-aged shoppers feigned indifference. Youngsters gawped, their jaws slack, foul language paused for a blessed moment.

If he didn't hurry he would miss seeing the car drive along the meandering tarmac of the cemetery. His favourite thing to witness: the hearse travelling under the boughs of trees whose branches met like lover's fingers—a bridge of leaves, black car driving towards the salvation of God's holy tenement.

Bouquet in hand, Maurice walked at a brisk pace and cut through a side street. More like an alley, with dancing refuse and crushed, empty beer cans. Maurice grunted his disapproval. Why did he pay taxes if the streets were so unkempt? Grumbling to himself he pushed on. Sweat beaded his brow. His chest tightened and his throat appeared to swell with each step he took.

    He rounded the corner and saw the church, hearse nowhere to be seen. Stomping onto sacred ground, Maurice made his way over uneven flagstones to stand hidden under the eaves.

A Thousand for One
by
M.E Ellis

The clock struck me on the head. Pain bloomed, spreading from the point of impact down behind my eyes. I lost focus for a second or two. A white fuzz shrouded my orbs before dissipating completely.

The hooded figure stood beside me, face obscured, hands inside the cuffs of opposite sleeves. I should have felt menace emanating from his person. He should have inspired fear within me, yet—he didn't. I was used to him bothering me.

"Did that hurt, young man?" he said, voice a whisper, breath that of sour graveyard earth.

I grunted, rubbed my head and squeezed my eyes closed. "Just a little."

"I should imagine it did. I didn't mean to throw it quite so hard."

"I did wonder," I said and looked at the figure, "why you threw it in the first place. Why you *always* throw things at me."

"Well, I don't really know myself. I rather had the urge to throw an object and the clock was the first thing to hand, old chap. Leaving one's clocks and belongings within my reach isn't good practice."

I moved away from the figure, side shuffling to my left. He shimmied along with me. I resumed my examination of the cadaver on the steel table. Murdered between the hours of three and four a.m., I knew. I sighed. So much pallid skin—bruises, broken bones; oh the wretched sights I see before me daily, their time snatched away before originally due. The body was that of a young man in his prime. University student type, all floppy fringe and expensive clothing. Reminiscent of Prince Harry, I felt.

"Chop, chop. Staring won't do him any good. Find out who killed the bugger, that's what I say!" He laughed, probably at the irony of his words.

I ground my teeth together, my back molar paining in protest. "I'm trying to find something that will *stop* the police doing just that, though if I get distracted and miss something... In the meantime, I'd appreciate you vacating the room so I can work in peace."

A gust of stale breath enveloped me and I suppressed a gag. I should be used to these smells, but his... No, I'll never get used to that.

"Well, that's charming! I come to offer my valuable insight and you rebuff me. Quite inappropriate behaviour, if you don't mind my saying so."

Did I have any choice? He invaded my personal space most days. Times when he didn't appear I could get on with my job. However, today was one of the days I obviously couldn't.

"If you're going to assist," I said, "then please observe. If something significant and of import catches your eye, then voice it. If you persist with hitting my person with objects, I shall have to report you."

His laugh carried to me on a breeze of vile stench. I continued working.

"Report me to *whom*? There is no one to tell!"

"Oh, I don't know," I said. "I'm sure *He* would have something to say about your behaviour of late."

"He? Oh, *Him*... Well, He can bite my behind for all I care. I'm not scared of Him!"

I blinked slowly to stem my anger, as if the movement of my eyelids alone would erase the sight of the shrouded presence.

He coughed. Thick grey phlegm landed on my wrist.

"Scene contamination!" I said upon a sigh.

"Did you know," he said, "that an average sized hummingbird beats its wings over eighty times per second?"

I inhaled deeply. "No, I did not."

"Or that some of them can flap their feathered arms up to three hundred times per second?"

"No, I did not."

"Well now you do. It's amazing the information you glean when on the other side."

He floated over to the instrument table, and my stomach lurched in anticipation. The last time he'd lingered there I received a stabbing from a scalpel. My blood spurted, though thankfully not on the body I'd been working on.

I leaned forward now to lift a stray hair from the cadaver's chest. I heard instruments tinkling.

"Please leave those alone," I said.

"Maybe I don't want to."

I glanced to my right. He touched every sterilised piece, his hands gnarled and knobbly, skin like brown scabs. He toyed with a pointed pick I used to scrape dirt from beneath fingernails.

"I wonder," he said, "what would happen if I threw this? Would I hit the bull's-eye if I launched it in your general direction? How good do you rate my aim?"

"I rate it very highly, though today I don't wish for a game of darts. Your offer to play is appreciated and noted. Recreation at work isn't my strong point. Finding evidence," I said, emphasising my next words, "on who killed this bugger, *is*."

The instrument clattered down onto the surface whence it came, and he

A Thousand for One

glided towards me within a second. He brought his hand up to stroke my hair, the crackle of his skin loud in my ears.

"One knock to the head is sufficient for today, don't you think?" I said, placing the hair I'd caught in the tweezers under the microscope.

"Oh!" he said, slapping his palm on his chest where his heart no longer beat. "You wound me so!"

I laughed in exasperation. "I think it is you who wounds *me*, but we won't dwell on that."

He slipped through the wall of the room. I hoped he wouldn't return again today. Continuing with the task at hand, I jumped a little as his head abruptly poked back through the wall.

"Just in case you think I've gone...I wanted you to know I'm still around. Watching you."

Not looking in his direction, though I saw his hooded head from the corner of my eye, I said, "As if I would possibly think you had gone. I'm not that lucky."

He harrumphed. "Are you asking for a scalpel in the eye, sir?"

"No, no. I don't think that's necessary today, thank you."

"Oh," he said before popping his hood back into the corridor outside the room.

He left me alone for the remainder of my current examination. I zipped up the body bag and prepared to push the steel table towards the fridges. He came back.

"Miss me did you, sir?"

"Not really. I've been too busy to miss you."

"Well, that's just terribly undelightful!"

"I don't even think that is a proper word."

"I don't care. If I wish to say something is undelightful, I will. And you... are *undelightful*."

The body stored in the fridge, I turned and walked to the sinks, planning to remove my gloves and wash my hands prior to scrubbing up in the smaller wash area outside the main morgue. Pushing ahead, he swished his robe-encased figure to face me.

"Where are you going?" he said, his voice strident with panic.

"I'm going to clean myself up and then go home."

I turned on the tap. And waited.

"But... *Please* don't leave me. I don't *want* to be here all alone with the dead people," he moaned. His voice, reminiscent of a slowing gramophone, sounded mellow and thick with unshed tears. Of course, he wasn't capable of them, though did an excellent job of mimicking a person with life.

I sighed, a great exhalation of weariness. Every time he visited me he hated to see me go. I walked to the main door, wanting to wash up and get home to a hot shower and forget the day's events. The night before, too. He, however, stood by the sink where I had left him, head bent in dejection.

"I want to come with you," he wailed.

"Oh no. Not tonight. I need a rest from you."

"But I... *He* said I had to... You *agreed*!"

I swallowed and closed my eyes, remembering the agreement I had made—a thousand souls in return for hers. My wife would be returned to me. Alive. I exhaled through pursed lips, my cheeks ballooning. I held up my hands in acceptance.

"Oh, all right! *All right*!" I said and closed my eyes. And waited again.

"Oh goody!" he said, the sourness of his breath reaching me before his spirit did. He next spoke inside me, much like my own conscience. "I'll almost be desolate when the thousand has been reached. I've become quite attached to you, old chap!"

His soul turned dark within me, the jolly demeanour vanishing along with my own essence. Four hundred more and I would be free.

He knew my thoughts and answered, "Yes, four hundred more. Still, not to worry, it keeps you in your job."

You Shall Be Heard
by
M.E Ellis

David stands facing the corner, his back littered with bruises. His dirty white underpants, all that he wears, sag. The elastic in the waistband hangs slack. David's shoulder blades, sharply defined by the thinness of his skin, shudder as his tears fall.

"Why are you crying?"

The boy doesn't answer; his words locked inside. Rendered mute by the atrocities he has witnessed and experienced.

"I would love you to answer me. Why do you cry?"

The shoulder blades rise and fall, the only answer David can supply.

Beige fingerprints litter the walls of this room—scuff marks and dirt upon a once crisp cream. The bare floorboards, slippery from years of use, lack the polished shine from days of old.

"If you would like me to help you, please nod your head."

David's sobs quieten. His shoulders cease their bobbing, and his feet disturb the dust as he turns around to face the one who converses with him. Weeping sores encrust the lower half of David's face. He lifts the back of his hand to wipe away the tears. Tears that leave clean tracks on his cheeks.

"Would you like me to help you, honey?"

The boy eyes the woman dressed in dark blue with a badge on her chest and a truncheon in her belt. And nods.

* * *

Cleaned, dressed, and fed, David sits upon a chair looking out of the window. Children play in the garden below but the boy does not have the courage to join in. Instead, he rocks and hugs his knees to his chest.

"Would you like to go out and play, sweetie?"

The slightest of head movements indicates the negative.

"Maybe another time, then? Here, take these colours. I would love you to draw me a picture. Can you do that for me?"

The woman in the white dress with the flowery cover-all leaves the room. David reaches for the pen and begins to craft his story. The woman watches through a two-way mirror.

The boy's tongue licks the sores near his lips. He concentrates, squints and twitches his nose. He selects three crayons, red, yellow, and blue. David completes his picture and inspects what he has done.

Inside a red heart, a lady with yellow hair wears a dark blue outfit. Walking over to the window, David hugs the paper to his chest, wipes away a tear, and smiles.

Safe. He is safe.

Manhunt
by
M.E Ellis

Cordons surround the house—white, the word POLICE emblazoned across them in blue. I stand in the rain and watch from across the street. I'm a nonentity, one of three dozen, unnoticed. Umbrellas shield us, the onlookers. Rivulets of water meander down the nylon, drip onto fingers that grasp handles. Hands frozen by the whip of the breeze, our gazes lock onto the scene before us.

"I wonder what happened?" fellow watcher, her face half in shadow, murmurs to no one in particular. That comment must run through each gazer's mind.

Except mine.

"Looks serious," says a man, comrade in the macabre act of morbid fascination. His woollen hat keeps his head dry. His two words perhaps echo the thoughts of the others.

A black van veers up to the kerb, gutter rainwater brushed aside by slick tyres, windshield wipers stopping as abruptly as the engine. Occupants vacate the ebony carriage. Rear doors unlocked in lazy motions, there seems no rush. Stretcher and bag carried, the cordon lifted. The door of the house gapes wide, pulled open by unseen hands, the men are swallowed by the darkened hallway, carrying the burden of carrying corpses.

"Someone's dead then." Stater-of-the-Obvious looks around at the assembly of the so-called concerned. Shivers, shudders visibly pass through us all. Fear and dread for them, excitement and adrenaline for me.

"Oh yes, someone is indeed dead." I shake my head in sorrow, my face—I hope—a mask of pity for the deceased. Were I to lift my gaze and meet this crowd's they would undoubtedly see the sparkle, stars and kaleidoscope images dancing, my eyes searching, alert.

"Speck we'll hear 'bout it in t'paper?" Old and wizened looking, isn't he a clever man, realising it will be printed for all to see while we are sleeping? His out-dated bowler collects rain in the brim, yellowed moustache obliterates his top lip. It's hard to discern where his 'tache stops and his teeth start.

I shudder.

A woman speaks. "Must have been a murder. Stands to reason, what with the screams and everything. I'm sure I heard them, but I went back to sleep, thought I'd been dreaming. Only I got woken up again, heard voices, you know, saw the blue lights through my curtains, and I thought to myself, 'Good Lord, whatever can be happening?' and, you know, I got dressed and came outside…and stood with everyone else…and…here we are."

Long speech there from Miss Wallflower. She now stands silent, wrings her hands like wet washing. She puckers her lips, shields her eyes with lowered lids, top lashes gracing her cheeks.

And the rain drips on, a steady patter that bounces from the pavement. All cheeks cold and raw, the north wind doth blow in our direction this night.

Collectively, our heads jerk up. Eyes forward, hearts beating. The black van men come out bearing their stretcher. Small body bag atop.

"Jesus H Christ, is that a child in there? The bag is so…small." Voice from an unseen face. I detect the lump in the throat, the compassion in the tenor.

"Aw…" in various tones, both men and women.

My eyes shift, unseen by my companions as they stare in awe at the sight before us. I watch *them*. Listen. Pick things up.

"They are going back in!" Wallflower, shocked. "There must be more!" Her eyes fill, her liver-spotted hand quivering against her thin lips.

Oh yes, there are more.

I glance around once again, take in the features of everyone watching. Stepping from the pavement into the road, I make my way across to the house. Under the cordon, up the drive, shoes crunching on gravel, and in through the door.

"Any luck?" says my fellow officer, face pinched and white.

"No, he's not out there." I sigh. Take off my wet coat, my sports cap.

Manhunt.

Biography

M.E Ellis is a writer of psychological horror/thrillers and chick-lit. She veers from the darkness to humour at the flick of a switch in her mainly insane brain. Editor for Wild Child Publishing and Freya's Bower, associate editor for Dred Tales magazine, book reviewer and author scout, she is a very busy woman. How she finds the time to write her own novels is anyone's guess.

Her psychological horror/thriller books include *Pervalism*, *Quits*, and *Quits 2*. Her chick lits include *Garou Moon*, *Charade*, *All about Brenda*, and *Liddy and her Other Half*. She also has a chick lit in the upcoming *Dreams & Desires II* anthology.

Currently working on the finishing touches of her psychological thriller novel Five Pyramids, she is also writing another psychological entitled In Her Veins. Add to that a co-author title with Faith Bicknell-Brown and another book, a non-fiction with her sister, M.E has enough to keep her busy for months to come.

Stone Child
by
Bernita Harris

Anytime they can't find a body they call me. Psi-crime detective, John Thresher, phoned from a place called Wild Man Mountain.

"Lillie, I need you here. Dress for rough country," Johnnie said

I blinked at the clock: 6:45 a.m. An urgent case, then.

Either the connection was crap or his cell phone was dying. He was breaking up badly but I got the essentials.

Her name was Henne Bjornsen. Eight years old with a crippled leg. She'd been missing three days and they didn't have much hope.

No hope, really, if he called me.

Talent is a curse. I hate missing children cases. I hate finding their bodies by their pitiful little ghosts, by the small specters that linger at the scene, as helpless as in life.

A photographer hired to take promo shots of the resort had gone missing too. That led one to draw certain conclusions. Not nice ones. I said as much. Static blurred Johnnie's reply but not the tiredness in his voice.

"Wait a minute, Johnnie. You're describing a straightforward lost child/abduction case. Not paranatural. Why are *you* there?"

Irritation came through loud and clear. "The word came down and I was available. This is an economically depressed area. Logged out some years ago. Nothing in the way of minerals. Her father's opening this fancy resort. Plans a string of them. Off-shore oil money, I surmise. Foreign investment. Tourism. Jobs. He has pull with the provincial government, I figure…"

I lost his next comment. Probably an expletive. He continued, "Anyway. I have a trainee with me fresh out of Police College. He's a promising Talent but underdeveloped at present and he doesn't have your range. I need you to wrap this up."

If Johnnie Thresher needed me I'd be there if I had to crawl. I was to fly, however, ASAP. Johnnie had laid it on. I stuffed assorted sundries into a small backpack and decided that Deep Woods Off insect repellent would be my protective perfume for this case. Anything that flies and bites loves me. It's the only time I think I'm sweet.

I heard a helicopter concuss the morning atmosphere on the pad behind the cop shop when I came through the front. Rhoda, the dispatcher, her brown eyes snapping, handed me a mug of coffee and a thin envelope. Pure mud, but I appreciated the coffee and told her so. She liked me a little better now that I was federally accredited.

Stone Child

"Thought you might need it since it's so early. Here's what I could find. It's not much. The gear the Sergeant requested is already on board."

The pilot wasn't inclined to chat over the earphones. We flew westward, the early sun pale and sullen behind us. After I read the slim pickings Rhoda had gleaned about the area and the business, I watched our tiny silhouette scuttle like a bug over the landscape, swallowed occasionally by the greater cloud-shadows that darkened the topography below.

Rough country, he said. Not exactly mountainous in spite of the name, but with rocky outcrops, broken ridges, and deep ravines. Worn bosses on the Precambrian Shield. The sort of twisted land that includes sudden swales, shallow soil, cedar thickets and snakes. A bugger to search.

Rough country, for sure. As we circled the long tongue of the plateau, I caught glimpses through a surging sea of mist of a single access road, lined by power poles switch-backing up the jagged slope, to link the lodge to civilization. Such as it was. Civilization, according to the map, was a tiny town by the name of Manitouis about fifteen miles down river where a white water stream fed into a finger lake. Miles away I saw the plume that indicated a small forest fire. Lightning strike, I supposed. Probably the little girl's Scandinavian name made me think of Thor throwing his hammer around.

I didn't know how good my range would be on this terrain. I operate mostly by line of sight and mist made it difficult.

Johnnie stood waiting, like a grim megalith, when we veered and hovered over the small landing field. Some cabalistic arm waving and the pilot set us down. I dropped out of the door and staggered through lingering ground fog toward him, saw his granite face relax in a brief smile. His aura flared golden before it returned to its steady dark blue. I imagine mine flamed like a supernova on seeing him again.

As always when we met I had the primitive urge to cast myself like a foolish damsel on his broad and manly chest. As always, I refrained. This case had carved new grooves around his nice mouth and hardened his angle iron jaw. Kid cases do that.

I took a deep breath and inhaled, along with several black flies, a familiar sweet stench. I looked down. A plastic and tarp-wrapped bundle lay on a make-shift stretcher on the ground between us. Almost small enough for a child. I turned and walked away to save my stomach and to hide sudden tears. Too frequently bodies lay between us. Like dead husbands. They don't do much for romance.

"No," John yelled over the continuous *whop-whop* of the machine. "It's the photographer. What's left of him, that is. Body badly mangled. We might not have found him except for the turkey vultures."

He looked up, and I followed his gaze. A pair cruised lazily, hopefully, overhead.

"Thermal imaging no help?" I ventured. I assumed they'd tried it.

"Under an overhang. The kid might be in the same kind of location."

Johnnie made a come-along motion. Another man, waiting by a black, two-passenger All Terraine, straightened and stepped forward.

"Lillie, this is Will Smith, my trainee. He'll fill you in. Will, Lillie St. Claire."

PC Smith, lean and lanky and stiff in an invisible uniform, appraised me, waiting for the inevitable gushy reaction to his name. Like Johnnie, he wore black field gear. I noted the twin streaks of silver at each temple that indicated Talent. Some people dyed their hair to hide it. For him, I supposed it produced just one more prejudice.

I nodded at Smith but directed my question at Johnnie. "You're leaving?" I managed not to bleat.

"Complications. Developments. Sorry."

They picked up the crude stretcher and headed for the chopper. I took the opportunity to dig out the repellant and spray myself liberally. As usual, I did a quick sweep of the area for resident ghosts. Nothing. I waited, feeling rather forlorn. Perhaps it showed. Instead of climbing into the waiting machine, Johnnie followed his young trainee back to me. He gave Smith a long steady look, then reached down a big hand. He brushed aside a long strand of silver hair loosened by the rotor wash and cupped my cheek, his blue eyes darkening to indigo.

"Take care, Lillie," he said. "I'll be back this evening if I can."

We watched in silence as the bird lifted and heeled away. Finally, we turned and gave each other a more thorough scrutiny. He did look like the actor, down to the ears and the thin moustache. I decided not to mention it.

"Why," I asked, letting down my hair to smooth it back into its usual tidy bun, "is Sergeant Thresher in such a big whoring rush?" I wasn't sure I liked being Chief Talent. More used to being support.

"Turns out the photog wasn't exactly a photog. He may be a part-time investigator attached to the PIS task force. Since communication from and around here is shit—even the two-way radios don't work well here—Sarge has gone to check it out and hurry up the autopsy. I'm no coroner, but we both noticed some anomalous damage to the body. Even though scavengers had been at it."

"Anomalous? Which means?" I asked around the hair clip between my teeth.

"Beaten to a bloody pulp." He watched to see how I reacted to that and seemed relieved when I shrugged. I could hurl my dinner with the best of them at the sight and smell of a mangled body but I don't heave at descriptions.

"What's PIS?" I questioned cautiously.

New acronyms emerged every month in this business. Governmental reaction to the sudden and inexplicable increase in various specters and paranormal entities was still in its infancy. While the bureaucracy struggled to control the various social and legal ramifications and complications, they produced some strange and decidedly ad hoc regulations. Sometimes it was hard to keep up. Still, after turning the phrase over in my mind, I wondered if he was putting me on.

"Protection of Indigenous Spirits. New amendment to the Immigration Act. Or Customs. One of them. I'm not sure which. Regulates foreign influx. At least that's the theory. Well named. In the wind, if you ask me." Smith grimaced and shook his head.

"Quite," I replied. "It's not as if too many people deliberately import paranormals..."

Smith nodded and smoothed his moustache with one forefinger. "Right. The Sergeant said you were a mega-Talent, full-spectrum, and an exorcist to boot and you're in charge. He also said my ass is grass if you so much as break a nail."

A *bodyguard*? Of course, Johnnie has "to serve and protect" invisibly tattooed on his forehead. It annoyed me sometimes. I wasn't used to it. Nevertheless, a dead agent was a dead agent and coincidences are suspect. I hoped Smith didn't resent assignment to a protection detail. His posture remained stiff and wary.

"You and him go back a ways, Ms. St. Claire?" He managed the casual tone well as we walked toward the ATV.

"You could say that. We met over a zombie," I said and wished I hadn't. Like any trainee, Smith might be eager for war stories, but I wasn't going to provide them. Zombie husbands intent on murder don't make the best memories. Memories can haunt you like ghosts and are not so easily exorcized.

He whistled. "Sergeant Thresher took down a zombie?"

"No—I did."

I wasn't surprised by the hint of hero worship in Smith's voice. I rather felt that way about Johnnie Thresher myself—when I wasn't unspeakably irritated by him. Like now. Johnnie went, perforce, by the book. I, perforce, could not. Paranormal activity doesn't particularly lend itself to set procedures and quantifiable evidence.

"So," I asked to change the subject, "when did you first discover you were a Freak like me? Imaginary friends who weren't exactly imaginary? Do you prefer Will or William? Call me Lillie, please. And where do we go from here?"

His shoulders relaxed and he grinned. "In order: Right on. Will, please. Thank you. Pretty name, if you don't mind me saying so. From here, we trust me driving an ATV down this bitch of a trail to the lodge."

"Any search parties still out?" I asked as I shrugged off my backpack, grabbed the roller bar and climbed in. "Visibility looked pretty poor from the air."

"Nope, called off. Men needed for a small forest fire east of here—you probably saw the smoke when you flew over." He reached into the back compartment and handed me a helmet. "They buggered off as soon as we brought the body in—and glad to go. At least they certainly gave us the impression they'd all sooner be somewhere else. Strongly."

"*What*? Why? I would have thought—a *child*..."

"Well, for one, we're on scene. For another, they figure she's dead, from exposure if nothing worse—and probably eaten. Fair number of bears around here they say. Certainly we saw lots of bear shit. Case closed as far as they're concerned. The other thing is that I'd say they were spooked." He ducked under a grasping branch to the other side and settled in the driver's seat. A squirrel leaped to a tamarack from a trail-side pile of slash and stumps and chattered at us.

He turned toward me and ticked off on his brown fingers. "One: all complained about feeling watched and followed." Will rolled a shoulder. "I have to say I felt that too, when the Sergeant and I were out yesterday doing ghost patrol. Two: high-pitched humming sounds. We never heard any of that ourselves, but the teams were pretty twitchy about it. And this everlasting ground mist is not natural, they said. It lifts for a while—like now—and then settles back in. They all had a bad case of *there's something out there*." He looked at me with eyebrows raised as if I was supposed to have all the answers. I wondered just what Johnnie had told him about my Talent.

"Interesting. Odd. The humming—it's called The Singing—reminds me of reports of an *Am Fear*—the Gray Man. He's a Scottish yeti. I'm surprised they didn't come up with rumors of something more in keeping, like a Skin Walker or a wendigo or even a *loup garou*..." The glimmer of a surprising idea took shape in my mind, but I wasn't sure what to make of it, lacking any other corroboration.

I mulled over his information, and then zipped my jacket against a sudden chill. "You'd better hope they just have overactive imaginations," I said at last.

"Oh? Why?"

"Because I wouldn't have a clue of how to deal with any of those, except the last."

He puffed out a breath when he saw I wasn't kidding, slowly turned the ignition and put the machine in gear.

A short bouncy ride over roots and small rocks brought us to the broad steps of the main lodge.

The complex was intended, according to the information Rhoda had collected for me, to be the first in a chain of Ultimate X-treme Adventure resorts, catering to the rich and jaded sportsman. For artificial primitive, it was very well-done. The setting helped. Spruce trees ringed the site like teeth.

I surveyed the stave-built lodge, the semi-circle of *hytta*-style log cabins with sod roofs opposite—I half-expected to discover a goat grazing on the rafters—and what looked to be a sauna under construction.

"That statue gives me the creeps," Will said, draping his arms over the steering wheel. "I suppose it's meant to be Big Foot. I guess the lure for the Adventure Lodge is customers can hunt for him along with the usual game. Like The Most Dangerous Game shtick. Tourism Ministry and Northern Development probably thinks it's a great idea."

Chained against a pile of stones in the center of the clearing stood a hulking figure of a hairy man with a club. I stared at the signature statue, the Wild Man, and made an instinctive mental leap.

"Big Foot? You could call it that. It's a wodewose, a troll, as they're commonly called. They're sasquach cousins."

"I thought trolls were little guys. Like gnomes."

"Not always. Forget Disney. They're related to ogres after all. Well, well, very Nordic. A little odd to see one here, so far from fjordland. We've found that there is often a correlation between local culture and the type of paranormal, and the ethnic background here is mostly French and First Nations. Trolls are clannish and keep to themselves—they don't usually attach to human families and migrate like banshees and some other Entities. Maybe your agent-photographer had reason for sniffing around. I can't wait to meet the owner of this place—and I assume that's him."

Coming down the steps was a big, bearded, fair man, almost as big as Johnnie, but far better looking by conventional standards. Standards, incidentally, which were not mine. He wore the usual north country garb and carried a hammer and a tool box. Obviously not the sort averse to pitching in and getting his hands dirty.

"Yep. That's Daddy-o. Looks at me as if he expects me to sprout dreds or my lip out to here." Will gestured and rolled his eyes.

I stuck my bug spray in my pocket but left my pack in the ATV. We climbed out.

"I heard a helicopter. Where is Sergeant Thresher?" the man demanded.

"Thor Bjornsen, the child's father. Lillie St. Claire. She's an accredited Talent. She's replacing the Sergeant for the time being."

Bjornsen ignored Will and the introduction. He took in my blue and black windbreaker, my jeans and regulation hiking boots, and frowned. He laid down his tool box, straightened and crossed his arms.

"Talent? I do not understand this 'talent'. I requested a proper police investigation of the child's abduction. A man is missing too, which is suspicious."

"We feel that finding the little girl or her body is essential to any investigation, Mr. Bjornsen," Will answered smoothly. "Ms. St. Claire's Talent includes highly developed Apparition Recognition."

Bjornsen scrutinized me again, less dismissively this time. "You are a *volva* woman?"

It sounded dirty the way he said it.

Will stiffened beside me.

"Did he just call you a car—or something else?"

"Relax. He means a cunning woman, a kind of sorceress. I'm the latest model anyway. But if he tries to kick my tires you can slug him." I gave Bjornsen points for nailing me with a cultural equivalent right off, but his instant recognition told me something too.

"You will find the child and the missing man?" Bjornsen made it a demand.

I raised a quick eyebrow at Will. He gave a miniscule shake of his head.

"I'll try."

"Your hair is silver, but your face is young—too young," Bjornsen announced, with nose-pinched suspicion.

Usually I don't meet the relatives of the missing—the emotional drain is bad enough without it. I didn't like him. I didn't like his red and black aura. And I especially didn't like his dismissive European arrogance, the kind that implied the Atlantic was a railroad track and Will and I clearly came from the wrong side of it. He didn't much resemble a frantic father, either.

Stone Child

Or even a resigned and hopeless one. And his manner, the frank hostility, expressed the opposite of welcome.

But to be fair, in his place I wouldn't have welcomed me. He couldn't pretend, as he could with Johnnie or Will, that I was anything but a body finder. I represented finality. In a sense, I was death.

All the same, I didn't like my thought patterns.

I hate missing child cases.

"It's a Talent Marker," I said shortly. "Will, before we head out, I need to see your maps of the territory covered. This is going to take some time, I'm afraid." Will nodded and walked off toward one of the cabins. I turned away and nearly tripped. A lean white cat flowed around my ankles and meowed, so I picked it up. It purred and snuggled and leaned into my hand.

"Nice cat. Yours?" I asked Bjornsen, who stood staring at me. One of his hands twitched, opened and closed, as if he fought to restrain some impulse. I remembered the *volva* had an affinity with felines, but I didn't see why that would bother him. Can't say I cared for the way his other hand tapped the hammer against his thigh, either. No, I wasn't welcome at all, not even as a source of closure. I narrowed my eyes and smiled up at him. Held his gaze until he looked away.

"The cat belonged to the child," he said. The child. Not "*my* child." Maybe it was a coping mechanism. Maybe not. However, I wasn't here to psychoanalyze the bereaved. I was here to find a body. Of a little child.

I *hate* missing child cases.

A green 4x4 roared into the compound. Bjornsen jerked his head in dismissal and strode away. I wandered over to the long barrow-style collection of stones to inspect the statue more closely. Entirely too realistic. I wondered if sunlight had petrified the wild man or if it had been the runic label carved like a name on the rock at his feet. Trolls were singularly impervious to most attacks, according to legend, but were particularly vulnerable to sunlight. I had no doubt somehow, this was a genuine artifact, and one imported at considerable expense. I put the cat down.

"Lady," said a polite little voice about the level of my waist, "have they found Henne?"

I looked down at a faded pink Dora the Explorer track suit topped by a small brown face. A very normal child, about eight to ten years old, not a ghost, but smelling faintly of wood smoke. She seemed an anachronism in these primal surroundings.

"I'm sorry, no. I am here to help find her. Where did you come from?"

She pointed at the vehicle. "*Papa* receives the garbage, he brings supplies, he does good work with machines. He lets me ride with him."

"Was Henne a friend of yours?"

The pink bows on her braids bounced like butterflies. "She had no *maman*. I have no *maman*. I gave her *le petit chat*," she offered, as if that confirmed their relationship. Maybe it did. One grubby and worn pink running shoe rubbed the animal's back.

"Did you two have any secret places in the woods where you played?" Kids sometimes knew—and saw—more than the adults.

Dark eyes assessed me. She looked down at the bouquet of trilliums clutched in her hands and skipped off to drop them at the feet of the Wild Man like a memorial.

On her return, she inspected me again before she offered, "Henne was not permitted to play outside. She had a stone leg. She didn't like the sun. I am called Heidi Thibodaux. How are you called?"

I am called at the death, I thought. "Lillie," I said. "Your father is waving to you."

She scooped up the kitten and danced off. I hoped her father kept her close.

Another dark-bellied cloud blotted the pale noon sun, drove a shadow across the compound and bled the color from the day. The wild face wore an eternal snarl.

She had a stone leg, Heidi said. Of course, it may have just been a child's expressive description. Will emerged from one of the cabins with a back pack and a shotgun and signaled. I cast one last suspicious glance at the stone man and joined him.

He unfolded a topographical map with a portion outlined in red and a smaller section in blue.

"The search teams covered this area. They figured she couldn't have traveled further with her handicap. They also searched all along the road out." He traced the blue section. "Sarge and I hunted over this portion yesterday. The guy's body was found here."

"Will, does Bjornsen not *know* you've found the photographer guy's body?"

"Un-uh. Don't think so. Not from what he said. He wasn't around when we came in and we went straight to the landing field with the body."

"I suspect that's not the only thing he doesn't know. Spoke as if he doesn't realize that both you and Sergeant Thresher use a degree of Talent. He didn't seem all that pleased at me showing up. Acted like I was an unpleasant smell back there. No one told him about your skills or that I was coming, I take it?"

"The Sarge probably just forgot to mention it," Will said innocently, refolding the map.

"I wonder why... What time did she go missing, Will?"

"Some time in the night or very early morning, according to Bjornsen. What child runs away in the middle of the night in this country?"

I looked back over my shoulder. While the handyman unloaded boxes from the 4x4, Bjornsen stood, legs apart, arms folded, staring in our direction. "A desperate one, maybe, Will. And the photographer guy?"

"Bjornsen said he didn't know, just that the guy wasn't anywhere around when Bjornsen discovered her missing that morning. The guy's gear was still in his cabin."

"Take me to the spot where they found the fellow's body. I think I should begin there."

"A game trail a few hundred yards down will lead us in," he said, loading the Remington. "It's not that far as the crow flies, less than a mile I'd say. I hope you're ready—in spite of your dainty shape—for a lot of up and down scramble. We go?"

"We go."

We started down the raw dirt road. Will began to whistle, watching me out of the corner of his eye. A cop thing. They always tried it on, especially with contract civilians like me. Like a test. Very melodic, cheerful tune. Teddybear's Picnic.

"Smartass," I said mildly. "But go ahead, if it makes you feel brave. Of course, we might not be able to hear anything pussyfooting through the bush behind us with you whistling...and I assume you're not carrying that 12 gauge riot gun because you want to play Davy Crockett."

He grinned and observed he'd need his breath for the trek anyway.

We both did. No wonder this was the last quadrant searched. The terrain ran dark and bedevilled the further we went. Rocks leaned and jumbled as if tossed about, forming niches and small caves. The trail led over rotting logs, through spruce and cedar thickets, under rock faces, edged along sharp drop-offs; while recurring clouds stole the sunlight, silenced the birds and dissembled the forest shadows. And always the acid smell of scraped lichen and churned leaf mould.

No specters haunted our way, however. But something watched us. I could feel it, and I wondered.

Will led me up a narrow ravine where we mucked over the slick, slimy stones of a small brook. We disturbed nothing but leopard frogs—and one long, lethargic hog-nosed snake.

Finally, he pointed to a shallow undercut in the ledge above. A faint sweet stench lingered here below the wind. I didn't need to go closer.

"There." He looked at me expectantly.

I shook my head. "Nothing. He didn't die there."

Will let out a breath. "I didn't see anything either. I figure he must have fallen somewhere and was dragged here."

"Or was carried," I supplied.

"Unfortunately the area got pretty well trampled by the searchers before we got here."

"Let's go further."

Upstream the land gaped open into a natural basin with slowly eroding walls twelve or fifteen feet high, hedged by bush.

That's where I saw him.

He slipped and scrambled down the rocky ledge, waving his arms, his mouth open. He fell to his knees on the soggy ground, reached out a hand, looked up, reared back as if to avoid a blow, and collapsed on the rumpled ground among the red osiers as if he'd been pole axed. Maybe he was.

"Will," I said and stopped dead.

I watched the scene repeat. No audio, just motion, the last heart-stopping event.

"Can you see him?" I asked and pointed.

"No. Wait, yes. Yes. A little fuzzy. I don't have your clarity. A small man. The clothes match those on the body. It's a recorder ghost, isn't it? Last moments over and over?"

"Yes. He died here. I think this is your agent-photographer."

We moved slowly closer. After we reached the apparition I reached out in an act of impulsive pity and *touched*.

Then I staggered blindly to a convenient rock and slid down against it.

"Lillie! What happened? You *glowed*. What's wrong? *Lillie!*"

The splotchy blackness impeding my vision cleared. Will knelt beside me, probably uncertain whether or not to put hands on a Talent. Johnnie must have warned him, or maybe he'd learned on his own, that you don't touch another Talent without permission.

I flipped a limp paw. "Be okay in a moment. Never heard his name. I should have asked. Stupid. It's easier with a name. I don't know why."

"Gerald MacAffee," Will supplied automatically. "You *glowed*."

"I'm an energy sink. That's what ghosts basically are, you know, a collection of electrons, though it's a lot more complicated. Be glad your Talent doesn't include that—you'd never dare touch a cell phone, you'd fry it."

"You mean you get knocked silly by electrical stuff too?"

"No, not this strong. A bit dizzy, but I fritz non-grounded stuff." I wanted to add that power always had a price, of one kind or another, but it sounded too pompous. He would learn.

Will looked over his shoulder. "Hey! He's gone! You *exorcized* him? Why did you do that? The Sarge would have wanted to see that sequence!"

No, Johnnie probably wouldn't like it, though he was more flexible than young Will implied. Johnnie had to be. He walked a fine line between established procedure and the intangibles of paranormal investigation.

"Sarge is not here. Will," I said, again fervently wishing he was. This case had developed into more than just finding a little girl's body. "Would you like to be caught in the moment of your death—repeating it over and over?"

He turned away and dug a bottle of water out of his knapsack and handed it to me. "I guess not. But isn't it—wasn't he…"

"I didn't destroy *tangible* evidence, Will, nothing the courts would accept as proof of anything by itself. Even Talent witness testimony isn't always accepted."

I gazed around the small corrie. There must be another trail at the point he came down, and there might be, among the fallen and tumbled rocks of this secretive, secluded hollow, some sign of what brought him here. Or of what killed him.

"But if there's any evidence to be found it might be here."

Another dark-bellied cloud dulled the light. Will squinted at the sky and then at his watch. "Temperature's dropping. That damned fog will soon roll in. We've a little time before we should head back. You know the drill?"

I nodded and climbed to my feet. We quartered the basin, side by side.

Will spotted a footprint first. A partial heel print, half-filled with water next to more broken and dark-spattered bracken. Maybe searchers, maybe not. We thought not. Will didn't think they had come this far in. They'd stopped at the body.

"Let's try the perimeter next. You go left and I'll go right."

Along the eastern curve, screened by a sumac, where a slab of rock made a niche, I found her.

"*Will!*" I croaked it, but he heard and came running. I tore at the rocks that half blocked the make-shift crypt.

"Wait, hold it, Lillie," Will said. He fumbled a heavy flashlight from his belt and dropped to his knees beside me.

Flicked it on.

One small frozen arm shielded most of her face, but I could see the small contorted mouth fixed in an eternal scream.

He reached in a hand to touch, gently, the small arm, and recoiled.

But I already knew. Stone child. Troll child. There never was a Henne Bjornsen.

"Geesus! That's not rigor. She's...What *happened*, Lillie?" In spite of the chill, sweat beaded Will's forehead.

"I think...*dawn* happened. Sunlight. It petrifies." Tears spilled over, and I swiped them away. Sometimes I grieve for the Godforsaken almost as much as for the truly human.

"There are trolls here, Will. Rock trolls, I suppose. Trolls fit the stuff you mentioned that spooked the search parties. She ran away, tried to reach her people." It explained the statue back at the lodge too, but I didn't mention that. It also explained why there was no apparition for Will or Johnnie or me to see. Paranormals don't produce them as far as I knew.

"Trolls? But how'd they get here?" He answered his own question. "I suppose Bjornsen brought them, somehow, along with his friggin' statue."

"They can shape change sometimes, as I understand it, Will, disguise themselves as natural objects, so the legends say. And legends are about all we have to go by. The stones on that cairn with the statue. Something odd about them struck me at the time. Didn't look like native rock to me—maybe that's how he brought them in."

Will played the light over the small stone figure again. "I thought she had a crippled leg or had a cast or something. Both legs look normal from here."

"Look at her feet. One's darker than the other. Like older stone. Maybe she tried before. Maybe he punished her and made sure she couldn't move quickly."

Something glinted among the ruffle of brown leaves. He carefully drew it out, stared at it with revulsion. A chain, like a dog's choke leash, tossed in after her. Not needed.

I looked over my shoulder to the spot where the agent had scrambled down the cliff, too late. Too late for both of them. He'd seen. That had been enough.

Will spoke my thoughts. "I wonder if MacAffee followed him, or just happened by later. Doesn't much matter, does it? He must have seen the proof of what she was. He could blow the whistle on the whole operation. That's why he's dead."

He got to his feet. "Unless these trolls did him?"

I shook my head. "They'd never stuff and hide her in a hole like that. They care for their children. And there's the chain. Steel is a ward. They avoid it."

"And we can't nail him for it either. Too circumstantial."

"No. And he's a rich bastard. There's law and there's justice, Will, and they don't always meet."

"So you're saying he used her to keep them in line?"

"Yes."

His gaze met mine. "Then maybe we should get the hell out of here?"

Stone is heavy. We left her there.

Another path did indeed lead away from the top of the cliff, a marginally easier one than the first track we followed on the way in. A good thing, because the increasing cloud cover turned the late afternoon into twilight. Soon, we waded through a mist that slithered and stretched like ghostly arms to catch at our feet.

Will tramped ahead of me, stiffly alert, carrying the shotgun at port. Once, where the trail twisted into another defile, he took a combat stance and swung the gun up.

"No, Will!" I said sharply.

"Something big moved over there by that rock face," he said.

"Maybe it did," I said in a milder tone. "I wouldn't be surprised if we have company, maybe had it all along. And maybe, if I can trust you not to buckshot my ass, I should take point."

"It's still daylight."

"I wouldn't call this heavy overcast daylight and not for much longer. They are mist-walkers and shadow-benders, Will. And now that she's dead, *there's nothing to hold them back*. So don't excite them. Let me by."

The way back always seems shorter though the mist clung like fur. We had not yet reached the tote road when a drawn-out undulating howl rose from the direction of the lodge.

"Re-call siren," Will said. "Something's happened."

We broke into a dangerous, scrambling trot. After we cleared the bush, the gloom barely lightened. The faintest luminescence marked the compound ahead. Will slowed and broke the shot gun, out of habit, I supposed.

"No," I panted, holding my side. "Leave it loaded for now. Please. We can't know what to expect."

"Suck eggs, Lillie," he said, exchanging shells, "I want a heavier load."

The siren cut as we charged into the clearing.

Mister Thibodaux's 4x4 was still parked in the compound. Mr. Thibodaux, his face set and carved like cedar wood, ran to meet us through the gray mist that spread and grew ever thicker. Thunder rumbled in the distance.

Heidi was missing.

The story poured out of him without need of questions. Thibodaux paced back and forth in front of us, grease-stained fingers kneading the upper arms of his doe-skin jacket, his voice hoarse from shouting.

He didn't know when. He'd been busy wiring connections to the back-up generator. A matter of urgency. He'd become tired of her prattle and told her to go play. His work needed concentration, we must comprehend. He'd searched the cabins and the entire complex and the bush immediately around the lodge. He'd even gone up to the landing field. He'd hoped she'd tried to follow us, that we might have met up with her, for she'd chattered that the lady would find Henne. Of a certainty, she claimed. Usually she was a good child and an obedient one. She had been very sad about Henne.

His shoulder sagged and he spread his hands in appeal. "Madame…"

"From your faces you were unsuccessful, useless," called Bjornsen, striding towards us, carrying a big portable lantern. "And now this. Another child gone. Three people lost." He no longer displayed any twitchy mannerisms; his face appeared assured, relaxed, almost smug now. Reprieved. I knew then Heidi wasn't *lost*—she had been taken. Or given.

Will and I looked at each other. He eased one pace away to a cover position. My play.

I moved to meet Bjornsen, looked him up and down. "You son of a bitch *bastard*," I said. I pulled the choke chain from my pocket and shoved it towards his face. I wanted to strike him with it. "We found her. She was your hostage, wasn't she? For their obedience! You trapped them, you brought them here as slaves, to be hunted down like animals."

He put the lantern down and crossed his arms. "So? That is a minor thing. A mere regulation. They are not human. They have enslaved humans. They are less than animals," he said and added, "They killed MacAffee."

"How," I said, after a long pause, watching his face as he realized what he had admitted, "did you know he was dead? You counted on her never being found, didn't you?" I went on. "You counted on MacAfee being blamed for abducting her, didn't you?"

Lightning briefly sheeted the sky, and a rolling rumble swallowed anything he might have said in reply.

The lights went out.

We waited, still as stone, in the moving feral mist, until the generator kicked in. In the weak illumination provided by three lonely outdoor spots, I saw we were surrounded. To my eyes, each crouching figure glowed with green and phosphorescent aura.

Thibodaux crossed himself. Will swore and snicked off the safety. Bjornsen staggered and stumbled closer to us.

One of them carried a stone child. One of them, a living one.

Stone Child

Another bent his head in my direction and spoke.

"Lady. We followed. We found."

He swept an unnaturally long arm and Heidi was set on her feet. She tottered towards us, her eyes fixed and vacant. Her father sprang forward and gathered her up. She lay limp and boneless in his arms.

"See, they steal children. The nosey brat is *bertagen*," said Bjornsen with a certain desperate and malicious satisfaction.

As if the irony of his accusation stirred them, the shaggy stone-age figures shuffled and ringed us closer. Eyes gleamed. Tusks gleamed. Clubs lifted. Some, I saw, gathered stones from the cairn. Not good.

"What's bertagen? Geesus, Lillie," breathed Will at my shoulder. "This is tight. This is very tight. Those are the meanest bastards I ever saw. And there's a lot of them."

"Mazed, mind-stolen, shocked," I muttered. "Don't fire, what ever you do."

Bjornsen turned to me. "If you are *volva*, you must know *seithr* and rune magic to keep them off. You must know the names to bind them!"

"Like Rumplestiltskin?" I asked.

His voice thickened and rose. "Do something! Night comes. They are vicious, vengeful. They are not placated. They have refused the child!"

"What do you mean...*placated*?" I asked. "As in blood for stone? Did you offer Heidi to them, hoping that would keep them off? Did you send her out there for them to find her?"

As if to underline again Bjornsen's claim about my Talent, a white form streaked across the gravel and meowed at my feet. I picked up the little cat and on impulse held it in front of Heidi's staring eyes. Her slack features tightened into normalcy. "*Mon chat*," she whispered and reached for it. "*Papa!*" She turned her face into her father's chest and burst into gasping sobs. For a long moment, the wails of a frightened child in the near-dark stilled all movement. There had been no "papa" near to solace the stone child.

Over her head, Thibodaux muttered, "Madame...there is little gas in the generator. The lights will soon fail. They flicker now."

I sensed Will strain to listen beside me. I heard it too. The distant *throp throp* of a helicopter.

"That's the cavalry," said Will, "but he'll never find the landing site in this murk. It's too thick for his search lights. If he tried to set down he might crash."

I knew Will was right. From above the land would look like a gray sea, spiked by the tallest trees like the masts of sunken ships. Johnnie rode on board that machine.

"Give me the shotgun, Will," I whispered, "and then grab Bjornsen's lantern there just beyond his feet before he thinks to use it. *Don't switch it on*, or you'll end up killing us all."

That sort of lantern usually emitted high intensity lumens, like daylight. Bjornsen could mow them down with it like a light saber—but he couldn't get them all and the rest would tear us to bits in a frenzy of rage. I had a better use for it, I hoped.

Lightning glowed again, but Thor struck too far away to be of help. A fine rain began to fall. Cold, like old blood. Maybe the rain would put out the forest fire. Maybe the lightning would start another. You never knew. Mercies are always conditional.

"Will, your flashlight. It's pretty high power. Point it toward the vehicles and lay it on the ground."

The shadows shifted uneasily away from the brighter beam and opened a corridor.

"When I say the word, get yourself and Heidi and her father to the vehicles. The cat goes too. You guys goose it to the landing site and shine your headlights on the field. Enough light should filter up so he can see where to set down. You understand, Mr. Thibodaux? Help is coming. You will follow PC Smith in your vehicle."

"*No*, Lillie," said Will. "I'll stay. Better you drive the ATV, and Thibodaux his own jeep."

"I can't drive," I lied. "*Get that child away.*"

"I will drive one," pleaded Bjornsen. "One is my machine." I rammed the shotgun harder into his back in answer and forced him one halting step away from the others. The trolls wanted blood justice. There was no way we'd all be leaving this site. They wanted Bjornsen and they'd take us all to get him. I had to gamble for the innocents. I doubted the chopper had enough lift capacity to take us all anyway.

"Think they'll let us go?" asked Will. Thankfully, he didn't argue. Voice of command can work like a spell. Or maybe he realized an older authority than law ruled here.

"I think so. They brought Heidi to us. They're not at blood rage yet. Not quite. We'll see," I said.

I reached out and touched the lantern. My aura flared into a visible, silver nimbus as I drained the battery power.

Before it could fade, I fought off the disorientation and spoke towards the semi-circle of hulking figures. I saw them flinch backward.

"They have done you no hurt." I gestured toward the trio of Will, Heidi, and her father. "They will go." I didn't make it a request. "Do you hear me?"

The leader bowed again. "Lady. I hear. Do not Name us. Four will go."

Four. Maybe. Another gamble.

I nodded to Will. "Go, now. Move it."

As both vehicles roared out of the compound, as the lights gave a final flicker and died, I removed the shotgun from Bjornsen's spine.

Bjornsen tried to run. He screamed. Once.

I stood there in a grey world among the moving, grunting shadows, listening to the impact of rock on flesh with a heart as cold and hard as stone.

Biography

Bernita Harris writes romantic suspense and urban fantasy.

A former forensic consultant in occult-related material, events, practices and beliefs, her stories explore the mythic in the mundane.

She lives in Canada near the Thousand Islands. She may be reached at An Innocent A-Blog (http://bernitaharris.blogspot.com/).

Anya
by
Stacia Helpman

Carly stared down at the positive pregnancy test she held in her trembling hands, terrified to tell Mitch the news. While waiting for the result, she paced back and forth in the hallway, praying that it turned out to be negative. In the year that she'd been with Mitch, he had made it perfectly clear to her that he never wanted to be a father even though she longed to have a child. She knew he'd be far from happy when he found out about the pregnancy.

She'd contemplated leaving town and returning with the problem solved, but she just couldn't imagine taking a life, no matter how small it might be. She'd even considered leaving him, but the last time she'd tried that, Mitch had managed to track her down at a motel and she'd ended up with a broken jaw for her efforts. Maybe if she swore to him that she would bear all of the responsibility of raising the child herself, he might allow her to keep the baby. After all, sometimes miracles happened. *Just not to me.*

She sat at the kitchen table and waited for him to come home from work. She'd prepared his favorite meal of pork crown roast with mushroom stuffing in hopes of softening the delivery of her news. A brand new twelve-pack of Heineken sat on a shelf in the refrigerator. Dressed in a Mitch-approved sundress that fell to her ankles and left everything to the imagination, she pulled her mousy brown hair into a ponytail that fell down her back and carefully concealed the bruises on her face from the beating Mitch had given her the night before. *I'm getting pretty good at that.*

She heard his truck pull into the driveway of the house they rented and cringed at the sound of his boots stomping up the back porch steps. She hurried to her feet to stash the pregnancy test in a drawer and greet him at the door. He practically ripped the screen door off of its hinges, and she stepped out of his way.

"Hi, baby," she said in the most cheerful voice she could, leaning in to place a kiss on his stubbled cheek.

Mitch ignored her, walked to the refrigerator, and grabbed a beer. He rummaged through a kitchen drawer until he found a bottle opener before finishing the entire beer and grabbing another. He sat down at the kitchen table and eyed his plate. "What the hell's all this?" he demanded.

She seated herself across the table from him and folded her hands in her lap. "It's your favorite..."

"I know what it is!" he shouted. "What the hell'd you do? You been screwin' 'round on me?"

"No, never. I love you." She held her breath and watched him remove his hat and run a calloused hand through his long, dirty blond hair, keeping suspicious green eyes trained on her.

He finally picked up his fork and shoved a bite of stuffing into his mouth. Carly knew he usually calmed down a bit after getting some food into his stomach. If nothing else, Mitch loved her cooking. "Tastes good," he mumbled around a mouthful. "A bit cold, though. Next time, why don't you start dinner a few minutes later so I can get a warm meal for once?"

She nodded her head. "Of course, I'm so sorry. Can I get you anything else?" He downed his second beer and held up the empty bottle. She quickly retrieved another for him and discarded the empty containers. She realized that she had better tell him her news soon before he got too drunk and became even more unreasonable. "Baby?" she started.

"What?" he asked, not bothering to glance in her direction.

"I have something to tell you, but before I do, I just want you to know that I'll take care of everything. It won't be a problem for you."

He stopped eating and looked at her. A scowl marred his face. "Dammit, Carly, would you quit mumbling and just spit it out already?"

She took a deep breath and blurted out, "I'm pregnant."

His eyes turned dark with anger. "What did you just say?" he asked slowly, enunciating each word.

"I'm...I'm pregnant." She chewed on her bottom lip, frightened by the expression on his face.

"No, you're not, or at least you better not be the next time I see you." He pushed his chair away from the table. Advancing on her, he took a handful of her ponytail and jerked her head back so hard that she had no choice but to look up at him. "Get rid of it or I will."

Tears filled her eyes. "Mitch, baby, I want to keep it."

"I don't care *what* you want." He slammed her face into the table; her legs rubberized beneath her. "Get rid of it or I'll do it for you."

Pain bloomed behind her eyes, across her forehead. Blood trickled from her nose. She lifted her head back up. For the first time ever, she struggled against his brutal strength.

"You wanna do this the hard way, do you?" He pulled her to her feet by her hair and threw her to the floor. She landed hard on her butt, and his booted foot connected with her lower back. He grabbed a knife from the butcher's block on the counter and squatted down beside her. Turning her over onto her back, he held her hands in his above her head. He straddled her legs and began to stab her in the stomach over and over while she screamed and thrashed about beneath him.

Anya

She lay still and he released her hands, leaning down to brush a kiss against her cheek. "Why'd you make me do this to you, Carly?" he whispered. "I loved you, but I told you from the start that I didn't want no kid."

* * *

Carly opened her eyes and blinked several times, trying to clear her vision. Some type of plastic sheeting covered her, blurring her ability to see clearly. Although panicking seemed like a really good idea, she forced herself to poke a fingernail into the plastic. It took a few minutes, but she managed to break through and free a hand. She peeled the plastic away from her face; cool air kissed her cheeks.

How long have I been lying here?

She looked up at the nighttime sky and saw stars, guessing that it had been several hours since she'd blacked out. A full moon hung above her, emitting enough light to see her surroundings, which consisted of a wooded area beside a shallow creek.

She slowly pulled the rest of her body free from the plastic that bound her and discovered her body was completely nude. She stood up on shaky legs and cursed Mitch for leaving her like this, for humiliating her. She shuddered at the thought of returning home to that monster.

Perhaps now is my chance to finally break free...

With his attack still fresh in her mind, she suddenly wondered why she felt no pain. *I must be in shock*. She moved her hands to her abdomen. Tears fell when she felt the deep, jagged wounds that covered the entire area. She couldn't imagine that the fetus she had carried could have possibly survived the assault. *How am I even still alive? And where's all the blood?*

"Neither of you were lucky," an odd voice whispered through her mind.

She jumped at the intrusion in her head. *Just great. Now I'm losing my mind on top of everything else.*

"Look down," the voice beckoned to her impatiently.

Her gaze moved to the ground at her bare feet and she saw the most interesting-looking chameleon she had ever seen. Instead of being green, its body continually changed color right before her eyes. Blue to silver to pink to black to gold. Every color of the rainbow, and some that she'd never witnessed anywhere in nature before. The stripes on its back reminded her of a tiger; stripes that also changed color, always complimenting the hues of its body. She couldn't pull her gaze from the lovely sight.

"My name is Sundro and I am here because the gods have smiled upon you. They are giving you the opportunity to make a significant decision.

You may choose to forgive the one who took your life..."

"My life?" she interrupted, fear almost choking her. "I'm...I'm..." She couldn't bring herself to say the word.

"Yes, Carly. You are dead."

It made sense, she supposed. "That's why I no longer feel any pain."

The lizard nodded its small head. "You may choose to forgive him and take your place among the gods, or you may choose vengeance and serve the gods for all of eternity."

"What happens if I choose vengeance?" she asked, seriously leaning in that direction.

"You will be transformed into Anya, the Dark Angel of Death, and will serve the gods. You will punish and kill all whom the gods deem necessary, forcing your victims to face eternity in the bowels of Hell. Your first order will be for the life of Mitchell Foley for violently taking your life and that of your unborn child," the chameleon explained. "Choose carefully, Carly. You will be unable to change your mind."

There is only one choice to make. It's my fault that my baby is dead before it's even had a chance at life. If only I had left Mitch sooner. I must avenge the death of my child.

The moment the thought crossed her mind, she watched the lizard in amazement. It turned black—blacker than any night she'd witnessed—and the stripes on its back glowed such a bright silver that she was forced to squeeze her eyes closed tight. She opened them again—the lizard had gone. Her senses alert, she realized that something else had changed.

She stepped carefully towards the bank of the creek and stared at a reflection that she barely recognized. Her long dark hair, now a deep shade of black, held thin strips of silver throughout the thick mane. Her facial features, while still her own, appeared stronger, almost frighteningly so. She noticed that the muscles of her lean body looked better defined, and an invincible power coursed through her veins. Her clothing had turned into nothing more than black strips of leather; black leather boots covered her legs from toe to mid thigh. Black and silver wings protruded from between her shoulder blades, a mixture of feathers and lizard scales covering them.

She stared at what she could see of the wings on her back in wonder and amazement, experimentally extending them behind her. Each wing stretched out longer than her arm's span; quite impressive. She slowly flapped one and then the other, surprised by the simplicity of it, just like moving an arm or a leg. Moving her wings faster and faster until she hovered above the ground, she thought about reaching for the clouds, and before she knew it, she practically *could* reach them.

Anya

"I'm flying!" she shouted, giddiness filling her entire being. For the first time in a very long while she felt alive and in control of her life. She found herself laughing like a little girl and wanted to feel this way forever.

She eventually returned to the earth and smiled wickedly. "I truly am Anya," she whispered, embracing her new identity.

* * *

Anya found Mitch at their house. She stood near the back door and saw him seated at the kitchen table with a cup of coffee in his hand and his cell phone pressed to his ear. She listened briefly to his conversation.

"The house was empty when I came home from work yesterday," he said. "Yes, I know, she's always waiting for me here after work... No, she didn't leave a note or anything... Please let me know if you hear from her, Mrs. Bennett. This is so unlike her, and it's got me a little worried."

How dare he use my own mother to try to cover up his crime?

Having heard enough of his lies, she pushed the screen door open with a wild scream and entered the kitchen, a storm of fury brewing inside her. She snatched the phone out of his hand and smashed it against a wall where it shattered into tiny pieces from the force. His eyes grew wide and his mouth dropped open. The utter shock written across his features pleased her to no end.

"I bet I'm the last person you ever expected to see again," she said, a vicious grin slashing her features.

"Carly? How...? What...?" Mitch stood quickly, trying to back away from her, but in his haste, tripped over the chair.

"I am no longer the simple, little Carly Bennett who let you beat on her," she snarled. "You made sure of that." She spread her wings to show off what she had become.

"W-what are you?" His voice held hints of unease and disbelief.

She wrapped a hand around his throat and dug her long, black fingernails into the tender flesh, hard enough to draw blood. She lifted him off of his feet and shoved his back against a kitchen wall. "I am Anya, Dark Angel of Death, and I have come for my vengeance. I'm going to allow you to experience all of the pain that you caused me and our child and so much more. I'm going to show you what it feels like to be abused and humiliated. And I'm going to take great pleasure in it." She closed her eyes and breathed in the scent of his terror. Better than anything she'd ever smelled before, almost metallic, yet sweeter.

She released him, and he fell to the linoleum. Reflexively, he brought a hand to his throat and paled when he came away with blood on his fingers. "I'm sorry, Carly," he whimpered.

"Carly's dead," she reminded him. "Soon, you will be, too."

"No, please, I didn't mean it."

"It's too late for you. Mitchell Foley, the gods have judged you and so have I." She bent down and lifted him up by the front of his shirt. She opened the basement door and pitched him down the stairs, laughing at the sound of his cries, at his body hitting each wooden step with loud thumps.

"Carly, please," he tried again, clambering to his feet.

She followed him into the musty basement and kicked him in his groin. He fell to his knees, face contorting in pain. Anya let out a gusty bellow. "I already told you, Carly is dead. There is only Anya."

He crawled on hands and knees towards her across the cracked cement floor. "Have mercy on me, Anya. Please."

She crouched down in front of him and took his chin gently between her thumb and forefinger. "You want mercy, do you? I'll show you mercy like you showed Carly and your unborn child." She slowly increased the pressure on his chin until she heard a sharp crack and pushed him away from her again. He screamed in agony, music to Anya's ears. How she wanted to hear more of that sound.

He dragged his battered body away from her to cower in a dark, cobweb-infested corner. Tears streamed down his face, and he wrapped his arms around himself. Something tightened in her chest while she watched him huddled in that corner, looking like a frightened little boy with cobwebs in his hair. Pity mixed with horror at what she had done to him already and what she still wanted to do flickered through her veins.

"I'm not like you," she breathed.

She turned away from him and ran up the rickety stairs to the kitchen, closing the door behind her. She stood there, trying to figure out what to do. Her gaze snagged on the grocery list that Carly had posted on the refrigerator the day before. She retrieved it and scribbled a confession in Mitch's handwriting. Returning to the basement, she shoved the paper and pen at Mitch. "Sign this and I will show you my version of mercy."

He studied the paper before glancing up at the woman Carly had become. "I confess to killing Carly and you'll let me go?" he asked desperately.

Anya shook her head and crossed her arms over her chest. "Not a chance. Sign the confession, and I will show mercy."

"I...I don't understand." He gently wiped his tear-stained cheeks.

"Last chance to sign," she warned, reaching for the paper.

"Fine," he said softly, scrawling his name at the bottom of the page. He handed it back at her and flinched when she accepted it, obviously expecting her to strike him once again.

"Don't move," she ordered and hurried up the stairs once again and out of the small house. She placed the signed confession on the driver's seat of Mitch's truck. Satisfied that someone would find it there, she spread her wings, glanced back at the house, and flew into the night sky. "Burn." One word and the house turned into a blazing inferno, burning fast and furious, sure to leave nothing but ash when it finally burned out. "Goodbye, Mitch."

* * *

Anya's new life handling the job of Angel of Death proved difficult, but she never complained. She'd made her choice and she would do the best job that she possibly could. Every day she sent sinners to Hell and had no desire to join them there. She lived a sad and lonely life, though—or death, since she had technically died nearly a year ago. Sundro visited her daily—her only companionship—but he always departed soon after he arrived, leaving her alone with her next order of judgment.

Some days, she asked Sundro what other angels did while she handed out sentences. His only response: "All angels make their own choices." On those days, she wondered if she would have an easier job had her guilt and anger not clouded her mind after discovering that she had been murdered. In the beginning, she thought that having the opportunity to wreak her revenge on Mitch would be the greatest gift in the world. After months of dealing with nothing but the scum of the earth, she no longer saw it that way.

Her latest assignment: taking out the parents of a young child. The girl's parents were drug addicts and drug dealers who took turns beating the five year old. Anya sighed upon arrival at the apartment complex where they lived, tired of dealing with the worst that society had to offer.

She knew the routine by now. The rules were simple. She could do to the offenders whatever she wanted, but in the end, the deaths had to look like an accident. It had been pure luck on her part that she'd decided to torch the house when she'd taken Mitch's life. The only other rule: only her assignments were allowed to see her. Should anyone else catch sight of her, the consequence would be severe. She'd never asked what the punishment would be; wasn't sure she wanted to know. Instead, she played it safe and allowed no one, not even her victims, to see her.

She reached the apartment that John Bishop shared with Lisa Williams and slipped quietly inside. The place appeared empty, so she waited in the living room for them to return. She looked around the tiny apartment in disgust. She had seen worse places, but the thought that they were raising a little girl in this filth turned Anya's stomach.

Ashes and cigarette butts littered the entire room, except the ashtray where they belonged. Beer cans and bottles decorated the room, scattered on tabletops, the floor, even on the couch. She caught sight of a couple of used needles along with razor blades and a white, powdery residue on a round table in front of the torn and stained sofa. Several paper plates stacked on top of the television set held the remains of unfinished pizza and chicken bones. A heavy odor of spoiled milk, stale cigarette smoke, and something Anya couldn't even begin to recognize clung in the air. She wondered how anyone could survive in this dump, let alone a child.

Only about twenty minutes had gone by when John and Lisa arrived. Anya let out a sigh of relief that she hadn't been kept waiting too long. Lisa practically dragged her daughter into the apartment by a thin, bruised wrist. The little girl looked like she hadn't eaten a decent meal in months or possibly even years. It surprised Anya, frightened her a little when the child turned large brown eyes in her direction. *She can't possibly see me, can she?* Anya didn't quite believe that she could, but just in case, she brought a finger to her lips and whispered, "Sssh."

Lisa released the child's wrist and swatted her behind. "Go to your room, Adhara, and don't even think about coming out for the rest of the night. Because of you, Mommy almost didn't get her candy. You're a bad girl."

Tears filled Adhara's eyes and she blinked several times, pushing the tears away. She ran to her room and closed the door behind her. A couple of seconds later, the bedroom door eased open a fraction of an inch, and Anya caught sight of a brown eye spying on the living room from the small opening.

John and Lisa pushed some of the trash off of the couch and emptied the contents of a small plastic baggie onto the coffee table. They each took a tiny white rock for their own and began to chop it into a fine powder with the razor blades, eager to get high without a thought to their daughter's well-being.

This is one killing I'm happy to take care of.

Anya leaned over the druggie couple and blew gently on the cocaine that they were so anxious to snort up their noses, transforming the illegal narcotic into something far more lethal and far more addictive.

Anya folded her arms across her chest and waited for them to inhale the dangerous dust. A sense of achievement coursed through her while the awful team of abusers drew the drug into their systems. They both ended up snorting far more than their bodies could handle. Blood slowly dripped from both of their noses, trickling at a faster pace with each passing second. It splashed onto the table, the splats amplified in Anya's ears.

Beautiful sound...

Lisa wiped a hand beneath her nose. She began to hyperventilate at the sight and amount of blood. John glanced over at her, fear evident on his face. He swiped his own nose. Anya sensed his terror as he struggled to breathe. He clutched at his chest and his entire body seized. Lisa began to cry hysterically before her own body fell into a fit of seizures.

Five minutes later, John Bishop and Lisa Williams were being welcomed into Hell, the only place that didn't mind how much they had sinned.

To anyone wasting their time investigating these deaths, it'll look like a simple cocaine overdose. I hope Adhara will finally be safe either in the custody of a relative, if she has any willing to take her in, or in a foster home. Either way, she'll be much better off than she's been with her parents.

Anya spread her wings, preparing to fly off with her duty finished. Adhara's bedroom door swung open, and the little girl rushed into the living room. Instead of running to her mother's side like Anya suspected she might, the child ran to Anya and wrapped her small arms around her waist. "Thank you, pretty lady," the child said. "Are you my new mommy?"

Anya stepped back and out of the young girl's embrace, worry gnawing her innards at having her suspicions confirmed. "Y-you can see me?"

Adhara looked up at her with an expression that seemed to say, *Duh.*

"How is that possible?" Anya glanced at the television set. Adhara had a reflection while Anya did not. She shook her head in disbelief. If she had no reflection, she should have been invisible to all humans, even children. She knew there were consequences for being seen by an innocent. Fear engulfed her, making it difficult to breathe and hard to see straight. She suddenly wished that she'd asked Sundro what the consequences might be. She *had* to find Sundro and explain to the lizard that she hadn't intentionally broken a rule.

"What's wrong, angel lady?" Adhara asked.

"N-nothing." Anya knelt down before the small girl and asked, "Do you know how to use the phone?" Adhara nodded. "Call 9-1-1 and let them know that your mommy and daddy aren't waking up. Don't tell them about me, OK?"

Adhara nodded again. "It's a secret." She gave Anya an angelic smile and ran to the kitchen to make the phone call. Anya disappeared before the girl had dialed the number.

***

Anya returned to the forest where she had first awoken wrapped in plastic. She always received her orders from the multicolored chameleon here. She called for him over and over in a loud, panic-filled voice until he finally appeared before her. "I have no more orders for you today, Anya," he told her, always speaking in her mind.

"I know that, but there is something I need to tell you. Something that I believe is very important. I don't understand how, but a little girl saw me. Her parents were the targets. They couldn't see me but the little girl could," she explained.

"That is most disturbing, Anya. The rules were made very clear to you."

"It wasn't my fault, Sundro. I swear it. I don't know how it happened, but surely the gods can appreciate that I never would have chosen to break one of their rules. Surely they will be lenient for a first offense." Sundro did not reply right away. Fear clutched at Anya's heart and threatened to suffocate her at his silence. "Won't they?" she tried.

"We will have to wait and see, Anya. I cannot assure you of something I do not know for certain. You must go before the gods at once to plead your case."

She'd never gone before the gods. She'd been judged once when Mitch had murdered her but had no reason to be judged after that. She'd always made sure that she followed all of the rules because Sundro had emphasized to her the importance of not breaking them. She feared the worst—that they would send her to Hell where she would be forced to face all whom she had sent there. "What will they do to me?"

"You will soon find out," Sundro said and transported them through the air to a place Anya had never visited. "Anya, kneel and bow your head. Do not gaze upon the gods," Sundro commanded, and she immediately did so.

I couldn't look at the gods even if I chose to…

The brightness of the room nearly blinded her, forced her eyes closed. Any fear that she had felt vanished. Serenity washed over her. She sensed no harm would ever come to her, that she could kneel here before the gods forever. She had no more worries, and no matter what sentence the gods gave her, she knew she would be able to accept and appreciate it.

"Anya, our lovely Dark Angel." The voice seemed to wrap around Anya's entire body like a velvet glove, the most pleasing voice she'd ever heard: a woman's voice, a man's voice, and a child's voice rolled into one. It brushed against her bare skin, the softest feather. At the same time, she could feel the power behind it—the most powerful voice in the universe. "How is it that an innocent has laid her eyes upon you?"

"I do not know. I tried to be careful. No one else could see me but her," Anya said.

"It is most unusual, Anya, that only the child should see you."

Other voices talked amongst themselves but Anya couldn't comprehend their words. Every so often she caught a word or two but nothing that made sense. Had it not been for the peacefulness that enveloped her entire being, her body would have been nothing but one tense knot. At last, the voices addressed her once again. "We have determined what has happened. The child, Adhara Bishop, is without a guardian."

"She will be put into a foster home, then?" Anya questioned.

The gods laughed, a lovely blend of a man's hearty laughter, a woman's soft chuckle, and a child's high-pitched giggle. "The child is in need of a guardian angel, Anya, not a human guardian." If she hadn't been in the presence of holiness, she would have felt embarrassed by her misinterpretation. "Sometimes," the voices continued, "an angel chooses a path that may not have been planned. When that happens, another path can be disrupted. However, at the appropriate time, the error is corrected."

The voices quieted. Anya asked, "What does this mean for me?"

"It means, my lovely Anya, that you are being offered a second chance, a second choice. You may continue your valued service to us or you may fulfill another much needed position, that of young Adhara's guardian. What is your decision?"

Anya didn't know what to say. She hadn't expected this. "I-I'm not going to be punished?"

Again, the gods laughed kindly. "We would never punish an angel for our very own oversight. What say you to our offer? Will you continue to be our Angel of Death or shall you accept your second chance? Choose wisely. It is not every day that a second chance is offered."

Before Anya could voice her decision, her world went black.

* * *

Anya awoke in a very unfamiliar bed in the middle of an unfamiliar bedroom wearing a pair of sweat pants and a tank top. The bright moonlight shining between the blinds of a couple of windows provided enough light to see by.

How did I come to be in a bed?

She turned her head, and her heart nearly stopped. Adhara Bishop curled up beside her.

What the hell is going on?

She sat up in bed and a stabbing pain in her head greeted her. She squeezed her eyes closed to try to alleviate the building pressure, and when she opened her eyes again, she smiled lovingly down at Adhara. All of her previous memories of Carly Bennett and her time of handing out death sentences had been replaced by new memories of Anya Bennett, the social worker's memories. Anya had taken on the role of foster mother when Adhara's parents had overdosed on cocaine and not a single relative had wanted the responsibility of caring for a child.

Anya leaned over and brushed a kiss across Adhara's forehead. The little girl turned sleepy eyes to Anya and grinned before snuggling closer. "What are you doing in my bed again?" Anya asked, drawing the child into her arms.

"Your bed is more comfortable," Adhara replied, yawning.

Anya ruffled Adhara's hair and laughed. "Get some sleep, sweetie. We have a big day ahead of us tomorrow."

"I know," Adhara said. "Tomorrow, my angel becomes my mommy."

Biography

Stacia Helpman lives in Northern Ohio with her older sister and her German Shepherd. Writing has been her favorite past time for as long as she can remember. She spent much of her time during high school writing about imaginary people and places and hasn't stopped since. When not writing the next great novel, Stacia enjoys quiet evenings at home reading the latest in fantasy and erotica or watching horror movies and singing karaoke on the weekends.

Double Omega
by
Lion Irons

In the first hour of the day, sometime after midnight, my sisters and me are blindfolded and literally led by the hand down the fire escape stairs on the north end of the house.

"This way," Mother says, as if we can see where we're going.

"Samantha?" one of my sisters whispers, increasing her grip on my hand. "Stop trembling." But I can't stop my body from shaking.

We silently descend what I judge to be three flights. On the lawn at the base of the stairs, creaks from rusty hinges filter through the darkness, causing my innards to clench painfully. In a chain of handholding, we are yanked into a cold, dank, and moldy-smelling cellar. The air invades my nostrils, causing me to cough on the dusty, stale, and musty aroma. Mother and her minions pull us through a series of narrow, interconnecting underground passages that exponentially increase in humidity. Vapor attaches on my skin, hair, and garments. Appraising the sound of the echoes that rebound off the walls, I imagine that we are in a large room.

Mother stops us and removes our blindfolds.

* * *

In August, seven months ago, I was a loner.

Within days of registration for the fall semester, the University assigned a second year student, Barbra Grove, to help me through the toughest parts of college transition. She answered questions, shared advice, and guided me on a tour of the campus. I knew immediately that this scholastic junkie would never earn my friendship. Barbra, a history major, with short hair and a lazy eye, marched me from the dorms to the library, to the snack shack, and to the abandoned wagon repair shop. We finally stopped for breath at Coleman's Dell.

Barbra turned to face me. Due to her lazy eye, I couldn't discern if she was looking at me or behind me. Disconcerting.

"Mystery hovers over the death of Frank Coleman," my trivia-rich tour guide said.

"Oh yeah? What kind of mystery?" I asked. Throughout the day, this girl's repetitive history lessons jaded me.

Barbra inhaled deeply and launched into verbal action, "Reverend Coleman was the University dean in 1911. At the time, college enrollment had faltered since the mine's production slowed and the town's economy forced families to relocate." Barbra's face seemed to light up, and she flung her hands before her in what I could only imagine to be excitement. "Coleman miraculously turned things around when he happened upon a generous supply of gold in this cave where he was investigating cult-like activity. Some say he was murdered by a miner who thought the gold was his. But I've read that the reverend was sacrificed in a satanic ritual... Legend says his body is buried in this collapsed cavern. Right here at Coleman's Dell."

I glanced away from Barbra—her eye gave me the heebie-jeebies—and focused on the pile of rocks and railroad ties protruding from the earth in a mound on the far corner of Baker Street and Fifth Avenue. Though the creepy looking gravesite made me curious, I wanted to explore other areas of the town. Besides, I needed to make friends and meet boys. My gaze drifted across the street. A maroon-covered stucco house with gold trim, paver-stone walkways, manicured grass, and potted flytraps cast a shadow on my tour guide and me. A sorority house sign that read OMEGA OMEGA grabbed my attention.

"Are you in a sorority?" I asked, knowing instinctively that Barbra was no sister.

"I'm GDI," she said and puffed out her chest.

"Gamma Delta Insignia?"

"God Damn Independent," she said. "Well, actually, I'm active in Pi Sigma Alpha, the National Political Science Society, not the type of sorority that you're thinking. Do you plan on pledging?"

"Yeah, looks like my sort of thing," I said and glanced over at girls swaying on a porch swing and exchanging serves in a volleyball pit. Beautiful girls—the type that look like the mannequins in designer department store windows—they moved in a fit of activity as if standing still would turn them to stone. The girls, in skintight, shiny black skirts and flat rope-bound shoes tied at the ankles, wore black blousy T's with OO in bold, loud, midnight-blue Greek letters. A few used compact mirrors to gaze at their own pretty reflections. Not an average appearance among them. I was dying to be an OO.

"Is rush starting soon?" I asked.

"No, it starts in the second semester."

"Not until February? Why so long?" I said.

Far from rolling her eyes at my question, Barbra appeared to relish 'teaching' me the ways of college. "The first semester is a quiet period. It allows students to familiarize with the school and the reputations of the different Greek houses."

"And the Omegas… What's their reputation?"

"Double O's." She looked across the street. A slight sneer graced her mouth. "Perfection. Perfect clothes, mascara, bodies, and grades. They smell good too. The girls that join become perfect, they start normal but return brilliant."

We continued to stare at the girls.

"What are the other sororities like?"

"Zetas are cool but their house is a dump. Deltas are funny, easy to talk to, and they party the most. I don't know, each house is different. You look like an OO to me, Samantha."

"Really? Thanks," I said.

"But I wouldn't advise pledging Omega. Last year, my roommate pledged OO and it was great at first. Something changed about her, though. Her appearance and attitude mostly. She confided in me. Said that the Double O's couldn't be trusted. Right before she left the school without saying goodbye."

"Why can't they be trusted?" Curiosity burned inside me.

"I don't know. The Greek system is a society of secrecy. They all have something to hide. It's just that the Omegas seem to hide the most."

"Thanks, Barbra," I said and immediately dismissed Barbra's lazy eyed warning. I wanted what those girls across the street seemed to have.

* * *

The first semester dread of classes and loneliness ended when rush started. I visited the double O house as the big hand struck the twelve on the first day of February, which marked the end of the quiet period. Girls waited on the lawn and porch distributing pink ribbons, selling candy, and chalking the sidewalks to promote a breast cancer awareness fund-raiser. As Barbra informed me, rush is a big to-do, like an outdoor trade show where houses replace booths, and sorority sisters act as vendors.

Although winter, it was a nice day to be outside. The sight of children politely begging for buttons and cotton candy—their parents handing out quarters—looked so charming it warmed my heart. Seeing families interact with one another, the way they belonged to each other, made me yearn to join a sorority even more. No prior description of rush activities had prepared me for this reality.

An attractive girl with full fire-red lips greeted me. "Welcome to Omega Omega. My name is Rene, and you must be Samantha." She pinned a nametag with Samantha Slone written in perfect calligraphy on my sweater.

"Yes," I replied, surprised she knew my name. "Nice to meet you, Rene."

She whisked me off to the side of the house to the double door entry, chattering all the while. "I'm a senior. Business major," she stated proudly. "A soccer star, too. And I was born in Romania!"

"No way!" I remarked. "I was born in Romania, too! My Aspen parents rescued me from an orphanage, brought me to Colorado and raised me in the comfort of America."

"Wow! What a small world!" Rene said. "Several Romanians attend the school of Mines and most of them are Omegas. I'm here on a Student visa. After graduation, I will return to my homeland," she said in perfect English.

Excited to have something in common with an OO, I sighed with contentment and said, "I would love to visit Romania."

"Samantha?" Rene brushed my arm the way one would stroke a kitten. I almost purred. "Rush has rules that are subject to the wrath of the Greek Council. Invitations to join on the first day are strictly prohibited, and I could get OO in big trouble if I tell you that we plan to extend you an offer to join. I won't tell you our plans outright, but if you are interested follow me inside and let me show you around."

Thrilled understates the feeling that rushed through me. My body almost fainted: my knees buckled, my head lightened, but I managed to grab onto a banister to keep me balanced. I held back the big smile I wanted my pale and unworthy lips to flash. Her invitation erased my insecurities, eliminated my doubts that I would receive an offer. "Please, show me," I said.

The French doors opened to a room of blondes and brunettes with sharp, obtuse cheekbones. Diamond studs in noses and brows, they batted eyelashes that hovered over blue and green eyes. The mix of sorority girls had two things in common—beauty and full fire-red lips. They smiled and welcomed me as if they'd expected my arrival.

The Omega house had a bright sterile décor, and I sensed an executive high-powered feeling, like the prestige of a daytime television drama. High gloss marble floors, and black, grey, and ivory walls made it look like a high dollar perfume ad. A stainless steel framed black and white portrait displayed a sophisticated and elegant founding mother keeping a watchful eye from above a baby grand piano. The furniture looked to me as if it had been outfitted from the Sharper Image, and I considered the stark contrast to the charming and warm stucco exterior.

Rene introduced me to Malinda, and together they escorted me through the house apologizing for dust and dirt that was impossible for me to detect.

Malinda slid her finger along a wooden furnishing. "This credenza is filthy but it was hand carved by our housemother, Antoinette."

"She hand crafted this piece?"

"She has many talents. All double O's have talent, Samantha." Malinda pranced close to me, adjusted the position of my nametag, and dusted some lint off my shoulder. "Samantha," she repeated my name deliberately spacing each syllable. Her pronunciation of my name sounded like she was serenading me. The musical tone of her voice put me at ease in an otherwise formal situation. "You have a talent with numbers, do you not?"

"Yes. I'm a math student."

"Math students do well in Omega Omega," Rene said, steering us to the steps.

Malinda smiled and said, "After you."

Upstairs, the bedrooms were neatly organized and carefully arranged to fit several girls in each of the rooms. In the stairwell, en route to the penthouse suite, party pictures had been professionally mounted—I assumed—in between composite photos of alumni members. I noted the dates on small plaques beneath each picture. Some dated back as far as the early 1900s. I had yet to identify a blemish on any of the active or alumni sisters.

After meeting three Romanian sisters in the penthouse who read me a Romanian poem, nothing could stop my desire to become an Omega. From the marble gas fireplace, the first girl held an antique book and spoke three phrases. The language was unfamiliar but the sounds burned inside my soul. The second girl retrieved the book and read aloud three new phrases that provoked my spirit. Perched on a rock crystal podium next to a separate glass-enclosed bookshelf the third girl continued without the aid of the book. By the conclusion of the third phrase, my destiny with OO had been sealed.

"Samantha Slone," the first girl said. "I'm Sabrina, this is Kia, and this is Carmen." Sabrina addressed me from the center of the large circular penthouse room. Panoramic windows with an unparalleled view of the campus, a half circle leather sofa, two fire exits, and stacks of books next to chairs and rugs made the room seem homely. "Have we made an impression? Do you want to be an Omega?" Sabrina asked.

**

Double Omega

Just seven months into college and I'm social like never before. After pledging Omega, girls help me sort the piles of wrinkled but clean laundry in my dorm where I have to live until initiation. After that I can move into the house. Now, I'm a part of a group when I eat in the cafeteria and I'm never alone when playing X-box—the "more than one player" selection is finally an option. Others join me for school rallies and student-center tutor sessions. In the third quarter of the year, my sisters comfort me when the stress of academics overwhelms me to the point where I close the shades on my dorm room window, remove my make-up, and curse my plain reflection. In the frost and breeze of winter's end, even my bike rides to class have changed from a lone gazelle to a pride of lionesses.

I've sewn the midnight-blue OO Greek letters on each and every item of clothing I own. Excitement surges in my tummy; the honor of true membership is upon me.

Initiation Friday arrives. Asleep in bed, I jolt awake by the sound of hurried footsteps and excited whispers. I open my eyes and rub the sleepy dust from their corners. Glancing towards the dorm window, I see the first light of the rising sun through the gap in the drapes as it struggles to pass through the heavy material.

Someone touches my arm.

"Get up! Quick!"

The dorm is still quite dark, despite the sun's attempt at brightening it. My mind tries to match the voice to a face but fails. I swing my legs out of bed and hurriedly dress.

OO girls lead me and my pledge class sisters from our semi-darkened dorm. Through the corridors, we tiptoe, out into the college yard. Four vans await us. Clambering inside the respective vehicles, we speed off. I adjust my eyes to the daylight and see that we cruise inside the city limits but on the outskirts of town.

I glance at the other two female passengers and recognize them to be my co-pledges, Heather and Charlotte. Heather is a math major and her class schedule is a clone to mine. Charlotte is the younger sibling of the sorority president, Malinda—both third generation Omegas. The driver, Rene, wears rags along with Sabrina, who sits in the passenger seat to her right.

Rags? Why the nasty clothing? Weird!

After a short while, a steel structure comes into view.

"Time to get out," Rene says.

Anticipation courses through my veins, an excitement unlike anything I've experienced before. I clamber out of the car.

"Here," says Sabrina. "Change into these rags!"

Lion Irons

Rags for me too? What the hell? Jeez, I wonder what the rest of the initiation is going to be like if we have to wear rags? Is it something that will ruin my own clothes?

A frisson of suspicion creeps up my spine but I shrug it away and slip off my clothing, trying not to get embarrassed at the fact that many other girls witness my disrobing. I keep my shoes on.

Once dressed, a sorority sister says, "Follow me."

A short trek finds me inside the empty structure. I take in my surroundings. The large vacated room has two big overhead doors and high ceilings. Buzzing lights dangle in-between plaster columns. Empty paint cans and used brushes are scattered about the concrete floor, which has been painted like a giant checkerboard, but in color. I turn and see my fifteen co-pledges huddled together in their rags with nothing to do but await further instruction.

Active members Rene, Malinda, Sabrina, Kia, Carmen, and Karen congregate in the corner, obviously going over the final details.

Rene holds a yellow index card, steps toward us, and reads from it.

"Have a sister check the tag on the inside of your shirt for a color. Match the color on your tag to the colored squares on the floor."

Heather checks my tag.

"It's red," she whispers.

I check hers, thankful it's also red. *Does this mean we are in the same group?*

Heather and me walk to the red square to join Charlotte, the only other pledge on it. We wait patiently in silence. My heart thrums in my chest, and I experience the urge to go and pee.

Rene looks at us. "You three, follow me and Kia back outside."

My frown must be evident for it hurts my brow.

"Get into this van," says Kia.

We climb into the van. Misgivings prod at my nerve ends.

"We're going to Baker Street," says Rene from the driver's seat. "Our housemother, Antoinette, is preparing a sacrament for the ceremony. But first, we have to go somewhere else." Rene starts the engine and steers the van out onto the main road.

The word sacrament makes me pause.

To take my mind off of the upcoming initiation, I glance round the van. Malinda, Sabrina, and Kia sit business-like in the first row. Heather and Charlotte sit to my left at the back, their heads erect. Their quiet poise catches my attention. I start to share my worries with them.

"Why are we going to Baker Street?"

Double Omega

"Shut your mouth," snaps Charlotte. "This is a serious mission!" Her tone is so curt and abrupt that I don't dare to reply, and I spend the rest of the journey with my mouth zipped and my heart beating painfully in my chest.

At Baker Street, we travel past a large house a good five miles, I guess, before coming to a halt.

"Get out of the van," says Kia.

We exit the van and walk while Rene explains the significance of the Double Omega history.

"The founding mother, Saint Rebecca, was a Romanian Byzantine Catholic. The Holy Eucharist or Communion is a fundamental tradition for Omegas." Her voice breaks the way voices do when talking and walking simultaneously. "In the Eucharist, we recognize that our mortal bodies can transform to perfection through the consumption of the Body and the swallow of the Blood." She stops walking, causing me to bump into Heather who also stops to listen. Rene waits until every girl stands still and every eye looks at her before she says, "Omegas make an exchange that is not merely for pious devotion but a sacrifice of our soul for a sisterhood that is eternal." We pause under the shade of a tree; Sabrina hands out berries, Kia passes a community water bottle. We sit Indian style in a circle on the dirt in an empty lot and meditate for hours. Girls relieve themselves in bushes when holding it is no longer possible. The sound of wind and the activity of insects keeps my thoughts company. I feel like I'm stuck at an airport without money for a flight.

After dark, I'm weary and bored. The solemn demeanor and hostile stare on the active girls starts to piss me off. Heather and Charlotte remain silent the entire time, and I don't know what to make of the initiation. By the glow of the moon, Rene stands first, followed by Sabrina, Kia, Heather, and Charlotte. I stand, but my legs are stiff and my back aches. The girls start walking, along the gravel path that borders the lot, so I stretch my legs and try to keep up. We travel to the Omega house. Five long miles.

Led upward to the penthouse suite, Heather and Charlotte join me in the room. Antoinette is kneeling in the center of the room next to a flickering lamp. I gasp and place my hand over my mouth; her face is neither human nor animal. Her jaw and cheekbones are misaligned and covered with coagulated blood. Raw wounds imprinted as if freshly branded with the Omega symbol take the place of her eyes. I stifle another gasp.

What happened to her? How the hell is she still alive?

The feelings inside me are upside-down.

I flip my gaze away from Antoinette and see a hooded individual sitting

on a chair to her left, quietly talking to a robin perched on its shoulder.
A robin?
This is too surreal…
Antoinette speaks in a solemn tone, "AhtnamaS nesohc neeb evah uoY."
I look at Heather, who stands as still as Charlotte; neither appear to be scared.
"AhtnamaS nesohc neeb evah uoY," Mother says again.
Each of the active members starts to chant Romanian poetry and song. Much time passes—faster than the beat of my heart or the race of my mind. The chime from a clock indicates midnight.
In the first hour of the day, sometime after midnight, my sisters and me are blindfolded and literally led by the hand down the fire escape stairs on the north end of the house.
"This way," Mother says, as if we can see where we're going.
"Samantha?" one of my sisters whispers increasing her grip on my hand. "Stop trembling." But I can't stop my body from shaking.
We silently descend what I judge to be three flights. On the lawn at the base of the stairs, creaks from rusty hinges filter through the darkness, causing my innards to clench painfully. In a chain of handholding, we are yanked into a cold, dank, and moldy-smelling cellar. The air invades my nostrils, causing me to cough on the dusty, stale, and musty aroma. Mother and her minions pull us through a series of narrow, interconnecting underground passages that exponentially increase in humidity. Vapor attaches on my skin, hair and garments. Appraising the sound of the echoes that rebound off the walls, I imagine that we are in a large room.
Mother stops us and removes our blindfolds.
My first sight is Antoinette. Coagulated blood sticks to the tears in her skin and she studies me without eyes. My face sours and vomit surges up my windpipe. I attempt to break my hands free from Heather and Charlotte's grasps. I tug, but they squeeze my fingers harder. I endeavor to look at my sisters; they aren't next to me—Heather and Charlotte's bodies unseen.
But I still feel their hands holding mine.
I glance down. Severed at the wrist but alive hands hold mine.
Oh my god, oh my god. What the hell?
I jerk my arms; the jerk used to rid one's skin of an unwanted spider. I scream and shoot for an escape but the oval room has no door and the hands hold me steady. Nowhere to run.
The vapor that attached to my skin, hair, and rags must have been blood. I feel it mix with the tears from my eyes. Shivers beset me; images from

a campfire to my left appear. Sights from a Romanian orphanage in the period from my birth project like a movie, autobiographical in scope. People famished like skeletons, babies with sunken, glassy eyes, children dying, collapse on the ground or lean against the wall. The stench of decomposing corpses causes doctors to hold their noses. Soldiers storm the grounds, firing at random. Nurses drag the wounded into a doorway; gunmen spray the bunk beds with bullets. One woman, shot in the stomach, knocks into three men that bleed a river of plasma on their way to the ground. A couple in sateen red robes and black sashes snatch one screaming baby from a crib. They carry the baby and run, their backs to me. A midnight blue double Omega is sewn on the back of their robes. Smoke devours the images.

Restrained by the hands, my body can't move. The room morphs once more. I'm in the center of a cave, a rosemary light intensifying my view of the cavern. A hooded individual with a robin perched on its shoulder takes a whip, tasseled on one side, and holds it in one hand in order to loop the other end around the other hand. This individual stands erect and ready—for what, I don't know. The robin flaps its wings and flutters from its shoulder-perch, suspended in midair between Antoinette and me like a hummingbird.

Mother grabs the robin and holds it firmly in her hand and says, "Samantha, join me in The Holy Eucharist."

Words escape me. I can't manage a reply.

"This is my body sacrificed for you," says a voice from the individual in the hood. I know that voice… Barbra Grove? Her hood shimmies from her head, and she floats to Mother and me. Her eyes appear normal; a soft, salient green. I recognize her despite her gorgeous changed appearance. Mother holds the robin steady, and Barbra takes the whip around its neck… And decapitates it. She squeezes its body, bleeds the robin into a chalice. With a rip of feathers and skin, she tears meat from its breast. Everyone present forms a circle, the bird passed to Rene, Sabrina, Malinda, Kia, and Mother. Each takes a bite of torn meat; blood smudges their chins.

Mother holds a piece to my mouth and says, "taE."

Repulsion soughs through me, and I suppress the urge to retch. Opening my mouth, I allow the raw meat to be placed on my tongue. I chew—tastes nothing like chicken—and swallow.

I return my attention to the circle. A chalice is passed around.

Mother lifts it to my mouth and says, "knirD."

I sob, the initiation becoming too much. "No."

Mother yells, "Return her!"

"Wait!" Rene begs.

Malinda moves next to me, whispers, "Samantha." Her voice chills my spine. "Look at Rene. Look at Kia. Do you know who you are? You said that you would do anything to be an Omega. Look at Barbra."

Barbra, beautiful and confident, makes me wonder. The severed hands release mine, move down my body, touch my legs, and grab my ankles. With astounding force, they yank me upside down. Like a snake shedding its skin, I feel my soul peel away from my body. It swirls and dances before me, takes the form of winter's mist. Floating, floating away from me, it seeps into the walls of the cave. Wholeness fills my body—I'm alive for the first time in my life. The hands lift me, pull me faster and faster through the air, painlessly through the roof of the cave. I rise through the earth until night turns to day, winter turns to spring, summer, fall, and back to winter again...

It's a nice day to be outside.

I'm dressed perfectly. The day is bright, the season winter, the start of rush.

A plain and venerable girl with an eager smile purposely walks up the pink chalked sidewalk of my home.

"Welcome to Omega Omega," I say. "My name is Samantha, and you must be Marta." I smile and pin a nametag with Marta Morgenson written in perfect calligraphy on her sweater.

"Yes," she replies, surprised I know her name. "It's nice to meet you. You have beautiful fire-red lips, Samantha."

Rae Lindley

A Day in the Life of Simplicity
by
Rae Lindley

"Wake up! Your time is here once again. To cleanse the world of the bile that dares to go against what has defined humans for centuries now. You are a part of the human race and it is your duty to keep in the boundaries of this world. It is your job to set by example.

"Citizen 52701, you have maintained the appropriate body mass of 22.15. If at any time during your duty you exceed this by the maximum restrictions you will be terminated on sight. Your duty starts now and will end in 12.5 hours."

Lyn reached up and touched the button on top of the machine cradling her cranium. She didn't have to open her eyes to see the man on the media bar. Today the media host had white hair and he wore a gray jumpsuit closely matching his aging, pale skin. She sat up, hearing the small media bar ascending with a hum toward the ceiling. The machine switched gears to begin its daily monitoring. She stood, forcing herself not to put her hand over her stomach. She went along with her morning ritual: crossing the dim lit studio apartment to the kitchen where she started the coffee machine, checking the media bar to see if it worked properly. In her mind, she planned the night to turn out like any other old work night, but in her mind she felt something big about to occur on the horizon. Lyn finally felt at ease working nights now. She couldn't remember the last time she saw daylight, if ever.

The small unit sat in the living room at a high volume. Various people popped up now and then to give orders for citizens to follow over the course of the day. Lyn found it funny that the small set once served as an entertainment device to pass the time. Now it served a better purpose: to keep order.

The stainless steel coffee machine beeped from the fridge and the glass door opened to offer her the hot cup inside. Lyn grabbed the cup and walked to the window. Her mind began to wander while her eyes scanned the busy city below. The change came not too long ago. The crime rate had soared to massive heights. Population lost control of their civility and eventually their sanity. The governments all around the world needed a way to control the population and to keep order among the citizens. Criminals weren't held in jails but instead they suffered the punishment of execution. Not long after, the formation of a mass police force was granted martial law and the complete surrender to the media began. Lyn had read short stories

A Day in the Life of Simplicity

about the past regarding the development of television influence. Even in the past, ads were created to influence consumer changes in clothes and lifestyles, especially with the people who were considered beautiful.

The media changed all of that by putting new laws in order. The constitution was destroyed; the Bill of Rights burned along with all the books ever written of the past. She scoffed. Who needs paper with words printed on them anyway? She saved time and energy pushing a button rather than flipping pages.

The modern laws and the way of life expressed the convenience of current living conditions and pertained to the age of now: 3015.

Lyn took a slow sip from her mug. She remembered one particular time when she allowed her feelings to overcome her conscious mind. A time where it didn't matter where she was or what happened to her as long as she remained close to him.

Her hand froze midway as she moved the coffee cup away from her lips.

Him...

She struggled to jog her mind to connect the face with the scent and touch of the man that still claimed her mind. Like all of the citizens upon entering the new laws regime, Lyn had most of her memory wiped clean. Still, she could never shake that feeling of a certain man's closeness to her. It never left her mind. Only blurs and small images remained, never clicking together to form a complete face.

At that moment she noticed her hand over her warm, taut stomach. She resumed gazing at the city below where she was to work in a few minutes. Time would take its toll with the child growing inside of her. Breathe in, girl. She opened a cabinet where she held her yellow liquid emotion containment fluids and poured it in the last drop of coffee. Lifting the mug to her lips, her brain already alerted her of the bitterness ahead. Once the liquid entered her bloodstream, she felt herself drained and her mind cleansed.

She stripped off the gray tank top she wore, drank the last of her coffee and readied herself for the night's work.

* * *

Vehicles of various sizes zoomed back and forth under the night sky. A handful of patrol cars lined the slick streets. Between pockets of stalled cars, the black sky could be seen with sparkles of stars mating in union with the city lights. Lyn stepped from her duplex. She smiled, feeling the rush of wind from the cars above kissing her warm face. Even then, she felt their eyes on her. Every building, every corner held a watchful eye.

As she drove along the city, she peered through the transparent dome cover. A slight hum of power roared to life underneath her. The vehicle appeared like an elongated oval shape that made use of electromagnetic fields to repel its weight above ground. She could barely feel the rush of ground beneath her as she veered deeper into the city. Minutes later, she came to a stop in front of a coffee shop and shut down the vehicle's electricity valve, still keeping the hover motion on. The dome opened and she hopped out. Her thumb tapped the mini keypad, locking the car over her shoulder; she passed the crowd of men and women filling the streets. All dressed in jumpsuits. Everywhere she went, Lyn felt like she was looking in a mirror at the different people that passed by wearing the same jumpsuit and hairstyle. She waited until the huge translucent chrome doors of the coffee shop opened and stepped inside.

"Well, well if it isn't the hottest cop in town. I was just about to hunt you down for some much needed quality time."

Lyn smiled at the dark-haired bartender behind the counter. He wasn't handsome by any means in the conventional sense but he did take her body to heights unimaginable, even for just a few moments every two months for their trysts. "I'm sure you can hold on for another month, honey," she said smoothly. "Besides, the others in line in front of me can keep your stamina a lot more than I can."

Richie laughed. "Maybe, but there's no one else I've had more fun trying with than you."

He licked his lips allowing his eyes to roam up and down her body. Her blue jumpsuit served as a second skin. A police badge with her citizen number on the right side of her chest set her apart from the other citizens, along with the holster strapped on her waist armed with a blaster and a pair of cuffs.

"The usual?" he asked.

"No, actually, I had a coffee earlier. Just give me one to go and an extra shot of Emotin. I have a feeling I'll need a good distraction tonight."

"Coming up."

Lyn looked around the crowded coffee shop at men, women, and a few couples. Others stood around conversing. A sharp pain shot through her stomach like a bolt of energy, causing her to wince.

Richie peered over his shoulder while he kept his hands on the coffee machine. "What's up? You alright?"

She forced a smile. "Yeah."

"Here."

A Day in the Life of Simplicity

He handed her the fluids which she swallowed immediately.

"Tell me, Richie. What if you were with a girl..."

Richie cleared his throat.

"Ok, one of many girls. And one didn't go through the cleansing. What if she became with child? What would you have her do?"

"Nah, that won't happen. No one's missed the cleansing or they'd be dead by now."

She stifled the oncoming shiver throughout her body. "I know, but what if it did happen?"

He turned and looked her dead in the eye. "I'd have to turn her in and let the world deal with her."

Lyn nodded in agreement on the outside, but couldn't stop her nerves from fluttering on the inside despite the intake of fluid. She tried not to think of what would happen if anyone found out. The idea was worse than the consequence inside of her.

The media bar sat high above the coffee shop register displaying a man in a gray uniform describing the weather. A woman wearing a gold jumpsuit quickly replaced him.

"Tomorrow, gold is beautiful," the media bar chimed. "Gold is in. You will wear gold like beautiful jewelry. This message has been brought to you by the Media Foundation for the New World."

"Here you go." Richie set the blue cup on the counter in front of Lyn. "I tossed in a few E's for you take to work."

"Put it on my credits," she said and grabbed the cup. She smiled and tossed the extra fluids in her pouch.

"You got it." He looked around the crowded shop to check the area before moving in close to her. "Listen," he began. "Why don't you put in a recommendation for us to be paired up a little sooner and we can work off some of those coffee calories all night long."

"Can't, Richie," Lyn said. She pointed at the blue police emblem on the right side of her chest. "I got work to do. Besides, I'll be working all of this off in no time."

She turned and headed for the front door.

"Hey..."

She looked over her shoulder at Richie and tried to ignore the raised eyebrow and suspicious gaze that appeared on his face. "Is there something you're not telling me?"

"What do you mean?"

"Do you know someone with that problem?"

She quickly shook her head. "No. If I did, we wouldn't be talking about it."

Lyn turned on her heels and weaved her way through the crowd of blue toward the front door. Out of the corner of her eye, and through the crowd of smiles and shoulder length to short-cropped hairstyles, one face wasn't smiling. Prominent blue eyes on a ruggedly handsome face peered back into her eyes, causing her heart to freeze.

"Excuse me."

Lyn looked up at a dark man towering inches above her. He nodded respectively toward her and continued into the café. She turned back to the blue eyes that still haunted her mind but he disappeared. Something about him felt familiar even though her mind couldn't place him right away. *Did I meet him before?*

"And now it's time to welcome another citizen into the world," the media bar boomed across the bright city. Lyn, unarmed, glanced up at the screen, then climbed into her vehicle.

A tiny red baby squirmed in the gloved hands of a doctor. "Citizen number 42597-6B. Remember, life is a gift given to each of you and every baby made in the media's eye. Support us—"

"Officer 52701," Lyn's radio interrupted. She set her coffee cup in the groove under the controls.

"I read you," she answered, starting along the streets.

"Suspect approximately five blocks from the coffee shop on the west end. Smells like a runaway."

Lyn pressed a button on the side of her steering device calling up a holographic grid layout of the surrounding area. Small blue human figures raced across the sidewalks, spreading out among the buildings. She zoomed in to one figure aligning himself with the walls of the building.

"I read him. I'm on my way."

She turned the corner and parked near the small alley. Slamming her fist against the right side of the vehicle, she waited until the small door to her right opened, offering her a handheld rectangular blaster. The dome door lifted, and she hopped out, feeling the cool air against her hot face. Already she felt her skin heating up along with her adrenaline awaiting the signal to charge up.

The alley ahead appeared like a pitch black abyss. She turned her right wrist up to face the sky.

"Come out, come out wherever you are..." she cooed softly.

Lyn stretched her sleeve back to reveal a small rectangular device strapped on her wrist. She gently tapped on the buttons bringing up a green hologram of the area surrounding her. One of the holograms hid between a

A Day in the Life of Simplicity

pair of clean blue dumpsters backed up against the wall not too far ahead.

"I see you," Lyn whispered. She raised her blaster to fire. An eye-shaped machine flew behind her and hovered right over her head. Lyn heard the man curse a few yards down followed by the loud thumping of his footsteps descending.

She turned down the blaster and sprinted after him. "Stupid media," she mumbled under her breath. She didn't have to look up at the screens overhead to know that her movements were being broadcast and soon his eventual termination would as well. She respected the media for showing what could happen if citizens turned against the system, but she refused to let it interfere with her bust.

Lyn turned the corner and rushed down the alley. A thin pellet of energy exited her blaster and then another. Through the darkness, his body fell with a thud against the cool concrete. Slowly she walked with one foot in front of the other, holding the blaster steady in her hands. With a kick, she turned him over and took note of the large hole that burned through his chest cavity. The spherical eye hovered above the dead body.

Lyn pushed a few more buttons on her wrist. "Citizen number 46597-9B has been dispatched."

She watched one of the dumpsters bolt to life and sprout a small hand to scoop the man up into its mouth. As she turned and headed back to the vehicle, another sharp pain jabbed in her stomach. Thoughts flashed in her mind like negatives on a camera slide. She held a baby in her arms, smiling, laughing. A man leaned over to kiss her and look upon the baby she held. The same man from the coffee shop. A rough groan escaped her and her knees gave out. She fell to the ground, breathing rapidly. A moment passed, then her mind was clear once again.

"I've got to slow down, I know," she whispered. "I don't want to lose you." Lyn peered down at her stomach. *Did I just say what I thought I said? Why do I care about keeping this unlawful thing growing inside of me?*

"And now we'd like to welcome another citizen into the new world."

Lyn forced herself to stand and head back to the vehicle. She climbed into the car and continued driving down the slick streets. The thing growing in her needed to be on the screens like a normal kid brought into the world. Not growing in her, overtaking her insides and damaging her body. This was unnatural. Her mind fell upon the man from the coffee shop.

"Officer 52701," her radio blasted, bringing her out of her trance.

"I read you," she said.

"There's a renegade approximately two blocks north."

"Copy that."

She hopped out of the vehicle and opened her diagram. The hologram shivered with movement as a blue flash appeared ahead and behind her. Before she could turn around, a hand grabbed her arm and a sharp object pierced her side. She screamed, feeling intense pain shoot throughout her body, causing her to fall to the ground.

"Oh, no," the man's voice said behind her.

"I can't...move." She remained frozen on the ground.

She looked up at her attacker to find him draped in a dark silhouette against the moonlit sky; she couldn't make out his face. He held a small rectangular handheld device that appeared like a 20th century calculator from the old world. She wished she could make out what he was doing.

"I finally found you," he said.

"I..." She tried her hardest to move, but she couldn't resist the electronic impulses spreading throughout her body.

Before he could answer, her eyes closed and she fell into unconsciousness.

* * *

Lyn didn't know the time when she awoke. She immediately reported the disappearance of the renegade back at headquarters. That evening, she forced herself to climb the tall dimly lit staircase to her apartment with the voice of the stranger haunting her mind. As she reached out to grab the doorknob to her floor, a large masculine hand grabbed her arm. She turned around and on instinct launched a fist that clocked the stranger square on the jaw, sending him backwards to the ground with force. She quickly aimed her blaster down at him and stared into the dark eyes of the strong-jawed blue-eyed man who tried to recover. She recognized him right away.

"I had a feeling you couldn't stay away," she said through gritted teeth.

"I'm sorry," he said. He struggled to get up while he massaged the side of his face. He nearly made it to sitting position before her foot slammed against his chest and pushed him back down on the ground.

"Not good enough for what's going to happen to you, buddy." She pulled her sleeve back, but the small scanner wasn't on her wrist. She looked over at him and noticed the scanner spilling out of his hand resting on the ground.

"What—"

"I can't let you call for reinforcements."

"What did you do to me back there?" She pushed his body hard against the floor. "I suggest you speak quickly."

A Day in the Life of Simplicity

"I just stunned you. Don't worry, it was nothing harmful. Something I wanted to do to protect myself."

"Good thinking because I would have blasted you on the spot if I had a chance."

"I know." He groaned, trying to free himself from her foot's hold. "Look, if you let me get up, I can explain why I'm following you without struggling for air at the same time."

She hesitated knowing she should have shot him five minutes ago. But something about him tickled her insides and made her want to go to him, caress him, kiss him, touch him. She shook her head. *What am I thinking?*

"You alright?"

Realizing her imagination was running away with her again, she slammed her foot on his chest before freeing him. She turned away. "I'm fine," she said gruffly. "Just tell me your purpose here before I change my mind."

He slowly made it to his feet and walked toward her. Without turning, she felt his closeness to her. Lyn whipped around and held the blaster at his temple even as she felt his smooth, pale face only inches away from her. Her heart raced beneath her chest. She smelled his scent and it made her weak with need. Her body reacted in ways that she couldn't explain, and she had to wonder why the Emotin wasn't working like she wanted, at this minute of all times.

"I want to be released," his deep smooth voice invaded her ears. "And I know you want that too," he said.

Lyn scoffed. "Do you know who you're talking to?"

"Someone who's been brainwashed into hiding behind the media's eye," he said. He stared into her eyes.

Footsteps echoed nearby. Lyn took note of his sudden shift in weight from one foot to the other.

"Things are going to change," he whispered. "You just have to keep your eyes open."

The footsteps grew louder. He turned and disappeared behind the darkness of the staircase. Lyn backed up against the wall as the door opened on the floor above. She held her breath and waited until the door closed. After the footsteps descended, she exhaled deeply. Opening the door, she thought of how far the world had come since the changes. With the media's control of human reproduction, humans were allowed to enjoy physical pleasure with anyone they pleased. Everyone went through the cleansing, stripping themselves of emotion and potentially dangerous free thought, choosing instead to give their DNA to the media for the pursuit of ultimate human perfection. So why was her breath taken away by this renegade who was a pathetic throwaway of humankind? Why did she want him so bad?

She entered her apartment and a sense of relief washed over her.

"Welcome home, Lyn," the media bar said.

"Thanks," she mumbled.

She tried to ease her mind to prepare it for sleep, but visions of the stranger slithered into her mind. Her thoughts reverted back to the previous images. She could feel his soft lips on her as he caressed her. His large, defined masculine body wrapped around her own soft, feminine body. His presence was still near, including his smell, his taste, and for some reason, she could still sense the imprint of his body inside and out of her. Fear soon replaced the calm serenity of their lovemaking.

* * *

The next evening, Lyn couldn't keep her mind on work. Part of her was grateful for the lack of renegades on the streets. After clocking in, she opened the door to the back of her apartment and began up the stairs once again. She reached the second floor and heard footsteps echoing behind her. As she turned, she opened her mouth to speak. A fair-haired man made his way up the stairs. He eyed Lyn suspiciously and moved out of her way, allowing her to pass.

Heading for the door, she shook her head. About to curse herself for being paranoid, she heard a voice.

"Lyn."

She whipped around and saw the stranger standing behind her.

Lyn let out a sigh before trying to catch her breath. Her heart beat rapidly beneath her chest. "I was hoping—" she stopped herself. "I thought you'd be here."

He smiled and she swore it lit the area up. "I wasn't sure you would, though." He eyed the floor entry door at the top of the stairs and at the bottom of the stairs on the previous floor.

Lyn pushed the fluttery feeling in her gut away. "Who are you and why are you following me?"

"My name is Spenser Dell." He moved one step up closer to her. "I've been watching you," he said softly. "I wasn't sure before but now I remember."

Lyn slowly backed up the steps. "What are you talking about?"

"They tried to make us forget," Spenser said. "They tell you what to do. Where to go. Who to see. Even who to kill. In this world, you can't think for yourself anymore. But I was stronger than that. I remember what the world was like before all of this."

"They know what's right."

He grabbed the tops of her arms and held her in a tight grip. He leaned closer to her.

"No! They know how to dictate you. And soon they'll be dictating the child you hold...our child...unless it grows up to be just like me. In that case, some other do gooder cop will be in your shoes and your child will be in mine, and I can't risk that."

Lyn slapped his hand away and reached for her blaster. Before she could arm herself, Spenser wrapped his arms around her, pinning her arms at her sides.

"Let me go! There isn't anything inside of me!"

"Yes there is! You're growing our child inside of you. I saw it on the readout that night in the alleyway. I don't know how they didn't see it before but we still have time to save it."

"How do you know it's yours?"

She felt his body stiffen behind her at the question and immediately wished she could take it back.

"We had been planning ever since we got married years ago before all this craziness. That's why I had to find you. They tried to make me forget everything, but I couldn't forget this."

She didn't speak for a moment.

Spenser's expression softened. "I know my own son, Lyn. And my own wife. I know you don't know what to do right now. If they find out, they will kill you."

"I know. I..." Her body grew limp in his hold, and she leaned into him. "I've had my memory wiped when I got onto the force. I don't remember anything, yet you seem so familiar. I can't trust my own mind. This is exactly why we need them. They know what's right for us. I am the primary one who hasn't set a good example."

"A good example?" Spenser scoffed, turning her around to face him. "Our duty as human beings is to reproduce to keep our race going. It's our natural instinct to connect with other humans emotionally. Not to be cloned and bred in a bottle just because our bodies need to stay under some ideal weight or height requirement. Your media has it all backwards. No matter how much simpler your life is. You can't change the fact that you've given up your rights in exchange for the simplicity. If you're not going to see that then I might as well stop wasting my time and go on my own. Is that what you want, Lyn?"

Her heart grew heavy as she looked in his dark eyes. She tried hard to fight the lump that rose in the back of her throat. The images returned but not like before. Memories of him returned to her and she could see them walking hand in hand along the bright sunny beach. His hand caressed her belly and he was at peace with her. She realized the man standing in front of her was the man she loved a long time ago.

"I-I didn't recognize you at first," she said, caressing his face.

"It's the facial hair growing in," he said half-jokingly. "I was careful to shave every time I saw you."

"Spense…I used to call you Spense."

He smiled and his face lit up. "Yeah, you did."

She brought him in a hug so tight she thought she would hurt him. He held onto her body close to his and it was so right. She felt the blind haze slip away and everything made sense again.

Slowly they broke from the hug and their faces turned toward each other as if a current pulled them together. They embraced in a kiss that started out slow then slowly grew into a passionate fusion of lips enveloping each other and caresses that struggled to bring the other closer.

"I missed you so much," Lyn breathed after they broke the kiss.

"I missed you, baby." He held onto her. "I have spent the last few months of my life trying to find the ones responsible for this. The ones behind the media. You know we need each other right now, Lyn. More than ever."

He placed his pale hand on her dark, smooth cheek and gently caressed her face. She remembered he used the gesture every time he sensed that she needed to feel calm and loved.

Love. An emotion deep within her heart that was indescribable, yet completely detectable. "I can't lose you again, Spense."

"You won't. I don't plan on letting you out of my sight anymore."

She leaned on his chest, fear choking within her. "They'd kill us on the spot if anyone found out. I can't risk us or our baby being found out. And I can't go back to killing innocent people. If I refuse to go in for work, they'd…"

Her hand fell over her stomach again and a surge of protection jolted through her. She knew he must have sensed it too once his hand covered hers.

He never flinched as he spoke his next words. "We'll go inside the main compound."

"What? Why?"

"I've been studying it for a few days now. Some men and I have been working together to find out just who is behind all of this. If we can shut down all the screens, we'll have a chance at changing this world and waking everyone up from this nightmare."

After a moment's hesitation, she nodded. "Alright."

"First, we have to go inside your apartment. There has to be some decoder devices they stock in the closets of these places. That may help us gain entrance."

She turned toward the door and headed toward it. As her hand hit the knob, her head turned to look over her shoulder as if something hit her.

"Wait a minute, they'll see you."

With a smile, he held up a small round electronic device with its insides torn out. Small wires stuck out like tiny appendages.

"Not if the security cameras are all shut down."

She smiled back and opened the door. The hall appeared unusually dark, and she knew once the government found out that this part of the building was shut down they would be at her door in seconds to find out the problem. She entered the apartment once she set her code. The lights suddenly illuminated the apartment, revealing two men standing before her wearing dark, thick padded uniforms and helmets.

"What's going on here?"

"Citizen 52701, you are under arrest for treason of society and your government. You are set for immediate extermination."

Spenser grabbed her wrists and forced her hands behind her back, setting the electronic cuffs around her wrists.

"*What?* Spense?"

"This was a test." He pulled her around to face him and she saw emptiness in his eyes. She didn't know why she hadn't seen it before, but she knew how the clones were tagged. The tag unit was the size of a tiny spec of salt; the color of bright blue hidden deep within his iris. It lit his eyes up to a clear bright blue shade. Bright enough to be visible a few feet away. "You failed. A shame too, considering how you were up for consideration of Captain of this district. We had high hopes for you, Citizen. But we needed to test your loyalty before putting you in such a high command."

He handed her over to the uniformed men who escorted her toward the door.

"No!" she said. "Wait! Why him? Why Spenser?"

"Easy. It was your final and strongest connection to the past. For some reason we couldn't wipe enough of the memory away even with the strongest memory wipe."

Slowly, she shook her head, trying to calm the fire inside of her that made her want to rip his head off. "How did you know all of this time?"

His demeanor remained calm as he looked upon her. He held his hands behind his back and walked with such elegance that she knew he went through extensive training under the highest command of police government. All of his previous mannerisms, all of the ones that matched the real Spenser to a tee, were thrown out the minute his true self had been activated.

"The embryo you are carrying was implanted with a microchip shortly before it was placed within you. We knew every second where you were, who you were with, and, upon my arrival, everything that was said."

"You can't take my baby," she said through gritted teeth. "I won't let you!"

"Oh, the child will be taken care of. It will be another proud citizen added to our society. Perhaps to replace the job you were incapable of fulfilling."

Slowly, he shook his head. "Still, our experiment did prove one thing. And that is a memory wipe is still a necessary device for this society to thrive on, but not the only device. You felt something toward this Spenser person that drove you to betray us. Make no mistake, that will not be happening a second time. You should be proud of yourself, Citizen. You are ensuring a perfect society through your efforts. And for that, we thank you."

Lyn's eyes happened to catch the small media unit hovering outside the windows. She turned to her side to peer out at the cold night with its bright lights and media screens planted all over the city. Her gaze graced every one of them, citing her as a renegade conspirator. She felt the sting of a needle within her arm and knew what was coming next. She could only hope that the embryo growing inside her would continue what she started. Before she drifted off to give her life over, she heard the last words that echoed within her mind:

"And now it's time to welcome another citizen into the world. Citizen number 42698-97A. Remember, life is a gift given to each of you and every baby made in the media's eye."

Biography

Rae Lindley is a young Californian writer/artist currently residing in Phoenix, Arizona. She has been writing since 10 years old, loving science fiction and fantasy since birth and practicing art since as long as she can remember. She has written the illustrated science fantasy novella The Eye of Alloria and the futuristic sci-fi thriller of the future Cimmerian City among many short stories, articles and essays on the subject of film, comic books and writing. A fan of David Lynch and Alfred Hitchcock, she also has a love for film and visual storytelling and hopes to keep supporting her habit of speculative films and books. You can learn more about her projects and work at http://www.raelori.com/.

Know It All
by
Rosa Orrore

Horror rushed over Sarah at the sight of her brother entering the House of Lost Souls. "Richard!" she called. "Richard! It's not worth it!" Tears streamed down her face as Richard disappeared around the corner of the house towards its entrance, oblivious to the cries from his family.

An average looking, two-story house, it sat back from the road. The A-frame, made of some type of wood, remained impervious to time, inclement weather, and natural disasters. The house had stood longer than anyone could remember. No one who entered returned. So, why did people go? The lure of gaining the knowledge of the Universe. "But what good was that if you never came out?" wondered Sarah bitterly as she watched first her brother, then his wife enter the house.

Sarah's mother turned to her father, "We must do something, Gerald! We can't just stand here!"

"I'm going in after him. You stay here," her father said and strode towards the house with determination in every step he took. Only briefly did he look back when her mother called after him. He shook his head in response and said, "I love you," then he disappeared into the house.

Her mother made a move to go in, but Sarah grabbed her arm, hanging on desperately. "No, Mother, not you too. I can't lose you, too."

"He can't do this on his own, Sarah. Besides, I don't think I could live without him." She shook off Sarah's hand and gently placed her hand upon Sarah's cheek. "Know we love you, child." Abruptly she turned towards the house and walked away...away from Sarah.

Sarah dropped to her knees, doubled over with the pain of her loss. Great shuddering sobs wracked her body. All was lost in one sweep. Angry at the world, at them for leaving her, she picked herself up and walked towards the house. What did it matter anyway if she followed? No one would mourn her loss.

Yanking the door open, she stepped into the house...into her worst nightmare. Screams of agony and roars of triumph saturated her head until she wanted to cover her ears from the pain. But the smell and the sights that met her eyes once they adjusted to the dim light were more horrifying than any she'd seen. The walls looked like human flesh with the skin peeled back and reeked of putrid, oozing blood and pus. Scattered on the floor were bodies, human and inhuman, in every conceivable state of decay, being devoured by rats, large, black beetles, and mice with glowing, carnelian eyes. She heard a shuffling behind her and spun to see an enormous beast with huge, pointed tusks growing from its mouth and hands with fingernails long enough to skewer a person, lumbering towards her. Blood-flecked saliva dripped from its tusks and dribbled down its bloated, fur-covered body, leaving small, wet patches on the floor.

With no time to think, Sarah looked frantically for some kind of weapon, anything, to defend herself. She stepped backward and farther away from the door. Something crunched under her feet. A shudder of horror rippled through her body and she glanced down. Her foot rested on the vertebrae of what was once someone's back. Not a fleck of flesh, skin, or hair had survived on the skeleton. Its mouth gaped in a silent scream, and its hand clasped a large, two-edged knife. Quickly, Sarah bent down and wrenched the knife from the skeletal death-grip, then looked up. The beast loomed close upon her. She could smell its fetid breath as it panted in anticipation of fresh meat and the excitement of the kill. A long, bulbous black tongue whipped out, licking its lips in anticipation. Its heavily muscled, long arms reached out to engulf her. Sarah raised her paltry knife to strike at the beast, aiming for an eye. A blood-curdling scream reverberated through the tunnel directly behind the beast. The beast seemed to recognize the challenge. Angry, it deftly spun on the balls of its paw-like feet to face this threat to its dinner.

In the dim light, Sarah could see a beast nearly the size of the one that had been about to feast upon her charging towards them. Not pressing her luck, she darted further into the gloom, nearly tripping in her haste to be away from the grisly battle taking place. The knife clattered onto the floor out of her grasp when she hit the floor. Her breath whooshed out in a painful wheeze, but she couldn't stop to catch it. Blindly extending her hand, searching frantically for the knife—her one hope of survival—her hand made contact with a bone. All thoughts of squeamishness disappeared with the will to live pumping through her body. She ran her fingers along the bone, grasping and trying to break it. It held. Again, she gingerly put her hand out to feel for the knife, edging it further and further away into the gloom. Nervous sweat trickled down her back, and seconds ticked by with the knife still lost in the shadows. Something skittered across her fingers, and she snatched her hand back. Wiping it on her pants, she reached out one last time and came into contact with the cool metal base of the knife. A sigh of relief slipped past her lips, and she pulled her shirt from her pants to cut a long strip from it. Silently, she affixed the knife to the end of the bone with rapid, efficient moves, making a primitive spear. It would do. She nodded her head in satisfaction.

A few seconds later, two screams rent the air: one of triumph, the other of death. She glanced back to where she'd just come. Through the red-tinged murk, she saw the outline of the larger beast tearing pieces of flesh from its fallen foe and stuffing it eagerly into its gaping mouth. All interest it had had in Sarah apparently lost as it devoured its enemy with relish, grunting and slurping in its delight. A disgusted shudder rippled through her body. Determined, she turned her back and continued into this house of horrors, her first test passed.

Her eyes darted back and forth searching the shadows. Sarah clutched her make-shift spear in readiness and cautiously made her way forward into the gloom. A staircase made of bones and hair loomed out of the darkness. Eyes wide, she stared at it in disbelief. The steps consisted of skulls and pelvic bones piled upon each other, while leg and arm bones composed the railings. Hair had been used to tie the railings together and decorate. She forged ahead, determined now to find her parents and to survive at all costs.

"Such pretty hair. Such pretty hair. Will look so good upon my stair."

Horrified, Sarah glanced up into the yellow eyes of another monstrous creature. It hopped back and forth in glee from one bony foot to the next. Pale green skin was stretched taut over an almost fleshless skeleton. White, fine hair draped over its pointed ears and swung back and forth along its shoulders in concert with its movement. The creature rubbed its hands in feral delight. Eager to sink its fangs and its razor sharp talons into the sweet morsel picking her way towards it, it began to rapidly descend the staircase.

With growing hysteria, Sarah watched the creature hop agilely from head to head, chanting, "Such pretty hair. Such pretty hair. Will look so good upon my stair." The creature lunged, arms outstretched to encircle her, its mouth open to take a bite. She thrust her spear upward through the mouth, piercing its skull. The body twitched in a gruesome death dance, gushing green, vile smelling liquid. Its life force pouring out, it twitched one last time. Its arms dropped. Swinging slowly like pendulums, the nails scraped the staircase in a macabre tattoo while the huge, unblinking yellow eyes stared sightlessly at her.

With shaking hands, Sarah tugged the make-shift spear from the creature's body, wiped the green stuff on its loincloth, took two steps up, then sank to her knees in reaction. She lost track of time. Suddenly, she heard a woman scream. Mother? Her heart raced; fear and hope warred within her. She leapt to her feet and raced up the stairs and down the corridor. Another scream pierced the air, closer this time. Doubling her speed, she spun around a corner only to see another beast, much like the first two, dragging a body away into the darkness. Rage bubbled through her breast. "Mother!" cried her soul in agony. Soundlessly, she charged the beast, spear raised and aimed straight into its beady eyes. Intent on its capture, it ignored her until she lunged, spear extended directly into the eye, through the brain. It screamed in rage, dropped its burden and reached for Sarah.

Twisting the blade brutally, she snarled, "Not this time, you bastard."

The beast crashed to the ground, arms flailing helplessly in an effort to stem the flow that erupted from its gaping wound. Sarah wrenched the spear out and stabbed the other eye, twisting around again and again. The arms stopped flailing and the beast grew still. Out of its mouth rumbled a loud belch and black blood bubbled up, out and down the side to make an ungodly, foul halo around its head.

She turned to look at the corpse now at her feet. It wasn't her mother nor her sister-in-law. Her shoulders drooped in relief. "Poor, unfortunate soul. I wish I could help you," she murmured. Even as the words left her mouth, she could hear the rats, mice and those grotesque beetles skittering in excitement in their rush towards this new source of sustenance. She reached out and gently closed the woman's eyes, then she twirled and sprinted quickly away. She couldn't watch them eat. She just couldn't.

Hours, battles, creatures, and levels she passed through melded into one endless nightmare in her search for her family. With each new test, her determination grew to survive, find them and take them out of this hellhole.

Splattered with gore and nearly overcome with despair, Sarah looked up to see a door shimmering brightly before her. She hesitated. Behind her another creature lurked; she could feel its eyes assessing how long it could feast on her. Her decision made, Sarah opened the door and quickly slammed it behind her.

Light seemed to emanate from the walls of the vast chamber. Made of granite, the walls arched towards a vibrantly painted, domed ceiling. Vines, flowers, and animals rested peacefully with humans, angels, ghosts, fairies, and other mythical beings. At the apex of the dome glistened a crystal the size of a beach ball. A tomb-like silence filled the hall.

"So, you have come," scratched a voice that sounded as if it had not been used for years. "Good."

Startled, Sarah spun to face this new threat.

There in the center of the chamber sat a being, not old, not young, male, female, but ageless and sexless, on a plain, unornamented throne made of pale granite. It glowed like the walls. The being had a serene, almost resigned, expression on its face.

"Where is my family?" demanded Sarah.

"You will know if you defeat me." The being threw itself off the chair and lunged at Sarah.

In reflex, Sarah brought the spear up to ward off the attack. It penetrated the being's breast, coming out the other side. No blood flowed, no sound passed the being's lips—only a smile flitted across the being's face and it whispered, "Free, at last." The corpse shimmered, disintegrating into swirling specks of light that danced towards the ceiling. Joyous laughter and singing resounded through the chamber, and the ceiling came to life and the images danced in rapturous abandon. Amidst the celebration of the soul's flight, a gentle waft of air brushed her hair with a quiet "Thank you". A blinding light shot from the crystal into the chamber, gathered the specks, and disappeared.

Sarah rushed to the door. Her hand grasped the knob, and she twisted and pushed. Nothing happened. "No!" she cried. Again she tried the door, and still it didn't budge. She kicked it, pounded on it, threw herself against it until her strength fled and she lay panting on the cold, unmoving floor. She was trapped. Defeat shuddering down her spine, her body and mind becoming quiescent, Sarah surrendered her soul and she drifted into an exhausted sleep.

An ethereal humming woke her. The chamber still glowed, but a brilliance illuminated the throne. It mesmerized her. Leaving her spear by the door, Sarah walked in a trance to stand before the throne's unyielding surface. What should have been cool granite radiated welcoming warmth. Unable to resist, she reached out a hand. Warm to the touch, it brought a smile to her face. She could hear her mother's voice scolding her father. Tears shimmered in her eyes and trickled unaware down her cheeks. Her will gone, she sat on the throne.

Bands of light wrapped around her wrists and ankles, strapping her to the throne. She looked up confused. From the crystal descended a column of white energy. It engulfed her in its purifying fire, transforming her. At that moment, she knew what the being meant. No longer Sarah, daughter of Gerald and Kay Blanchard, she became Know-It-All, the guardian of the Universe. Trapped in this chamber with the answers to the Universe, she would wait in silent exile until the next hapless person came along and defeated her. Only then would she be free.

The humming ceased. The transformation completed, Sarah and Know-It-All were one.

Know It All

Rising calmly, resigned to its fate, Know-It-All walked to where the spear lay, retrieved it, turned to the throne and sat. There it would await its release.

Biography

Rosa Orrore is a pen name used by Marci Baun. Rosa began her existence in 1999 at the inception of Wild Child Publishing's magazine division when Wild Child first began. Her few and far between stories helped "fill" some of the pages. However, after a few issues, it was unnecessary for Ms. Baun to write for more than pleasure. This particular story was inspired by one of Ms. Baun's many childhood nightmares. It has been reworked for this anthology from its original incarnation. Rosa Orrore has since retired and has perhaps four stories to her name as Ms. Baun has very little time for writing beyond editing advice and email these days. To find out more about her, you can visit http://www.wildchildpublishing.com/.

The Surprise
by
Amanda Tieman

Jason jumped out of his cab, crossed the lot of Tanner Shipping, and walked into the main office.

Ron, his boss, looked back over his shoulder from stuffing the filing cabinet. "Hey, Jason. Did you finish that last run of pickup and deliveries?"

"Yeah, I just got back from Home Depot, it was my last stop." Jason rubbed his hands over his brown flattop. "The guys on the dock are unloading my trailer right now. What else do we have going out, Ron, anything?"

Ron closed the filing cabinet and leaned back on it. He crossed his arms over his chest, and Jason smiled inwardly at the sight of his boss's beer gut. "No, it's been a surprisingly slow day for a Friday. You can head home, spend some time with your daughter."

"I'd like to, but she has other plans. I'll get some R&R instead."

"You're not letting her visit that mother of hers, are you? Not after what happened in January." Ron's brow knitted with concern.

"No, of course not! Besides, Maggie's not allowed visitors at this stage in rehab, even if I *did* want to take Naomi to see her. She's got an overnight birthday party." Jason hooked his thumbs in his pants pockets.

"Good thing. Well, I'd better get back to it." Ron reached for another set of files and opened a new drawer. "We'll see you on Monday, Jason."

"Later, Ron. Oh, and don't do anything I wouldn't do!"

Jason heard Ron cackle as he left the office and made his way to the men's room to wash the bit of grime off his hands before heading out of the door to his Blazer.

Ron must have been momentarily out of his mind to think that I'd take Naomi to visit Maggie.

Jason shook his head. It would only take one look at the once new Blazer to figure out that while Maggie was Naomi's biological mother, she was in no way fit to be anyone's mother in the emotional sense.

She surely beat the hell out of my ride. Meth-head. Practically brand new when I got it. Now look at it. Looks like it came off second best in a match against one of those crazy contraptions they're always building on that show on the Discovery channel, Monster Garage.

Jason stood looking at his Blazer. The dark blue paint bore hideous scratches, the body covered in dents ranging from the size of a quarter to the size of a small cantaloupe. He'd been able to pound out some of the more major dents, but the paint betrayed his efforts.

Paint's starting to flake and peel. Jason sighed. *To hell with it. No sense in lingering on unpleasant thoughts. If I get my ass moving instead of standing here staring at the Blazer thinking about crap, I can take Naomi for an ice cream cone from Dairy Queen before I take her to the birthday party.*

Jason climbed into his SUV and gunned the engine. Popping in his favorite Jimmy Buffett CD, he cruised through town towards Naomi's school enjoying Jimmy's relaxed beat and self-indulgent lyrics. The school came into view in no time, and he scanned the lot for the day care van. He had no trouble spotting it since the van was silver with handprints in primary colors all along the sides.

He parked the Blazer, snuck up to the van and rapped on the window. Jill, the day care coordinator, jumped in her seat, startled. She turned to the window, smiled at Jason, and opened the door. "Taking Naomi early today?"

"Yeah. She's got a birthday party to go to."

Laughing, Jill rolled her eyes. "Don't I know it! That's all she's talked about this week." She tweaked a blonde curl behind her ear and tugged at the hem of her baby blue sweater. She lowered her voice. "How's everything going?"

"It's been going pretty good, all things considered," Jason replied with an unconscious glance at his Blazer. "These rug rats drivin' you crazy yet?"

"Dear, you made one seriously wrong assumption on that one." Jill tapped the side of her head with an index finger. "You have to be sane in the first place before you can ever go crazy, and I'm pretty sure I've never had claim to that one."

"Probably not. Well, hell, I *know* not," Jason laughed, paused for a moment, and said, "You know, Jill, you've been a great help the last couple of months. I'm not sure that I could have made it without you."

"Don't give me too much credit; I was just being a friend. I'm sure you'd have managed without me."

The school bell clanged, cutting off their conversation and signaling an onslaught of pint-sized pandemonium.

"That's my cue," Jason said. He gave Jill a wink. "See ya' Monday."

"Later, Jason." Jill chewed her lower lip and added, "Take care of yourself."

"I will, and you do the same!"

Jason headed to the Blazer to wait for Naomi, but he didn't have to wait long. She exploded from the building with a herd of children. Spotting the

The Surprise

Blazer, she came at a full run with her blonde pigtails bobbing and her Harry Potter backpack flailing from one arm.

My God, she looks so much like Maggie. Her blonde hair and that small frame. Jason smiled; pain constricted his chest. *Her smile reminds me of Maggie's when we first met.*

Naomi shouted, "Daddy!" Looking at Jason she balled her hands into fists and put them on her hips. "Aren't you s'posed to be at work?"

"Yup, but an alien spacecraft came and got all the stuff I was supposed to deliver and took it to their home planet to do a bunch of tests on it." Jason gave Naomi a grin and winked. "They said it would take all weekend and that I could go home."

"C'mon, I know aliens don't take your stuff for tests," she countered. Naomi wrinkled her nose and grinned.

Maybe things really will work out, Jason thought. *I'm actually feeling better and she seems to be, too.*

"What do you think about grabbing an ice cream cone before the party? I'd like to hear about your day."

"Yeah!" Naomi jumped up and down and clapped her hands.

Thank God Dairy Queen is only five minutes from the school, Jason thought.

Naomi had chosen the music this time; the latest CD by Hillary Duff.

Jason looked around the Dairy Queen. *Good, it's not busy. We can have plenty of time to sit and talk.*

He walked up to the counter and placed their order (a pineapple shake for him, a chocolate dip cone for her) while Naomi ran to the back of the store past an elderly couple munching sundaes and enjoying the mountains. Naomi plopped into a booth on the street side. Handing Naomi her cone and a stack of napkins, Jason said, "How was school?"

Naomi took a bite of her cone before answering. Face already covered in chocolate, Naomi's eyes lit up. "Alex and Ben got in a fight today! Alex pushed Ben down 'cos he took his swing." Her eyebrows came together. "That wasn't very nice."

"No, it wasn't." Jason worked to keep a serious face.

"Oh, and guess what!" Naomi rushed on without waiting for a reply. "Lily threw up in the trash can and it was *so* gross! And she had to go home."

I could have done without that information. Jason smiled. "So what did you do in school today?"

"Nothing," Naomi replied before attacking her cone again.

"Oh, so you just sat at your table and stared at the walls?"

"No, but we did the same stuff we always do." She gave her face a half-hearted wipe with a napkin.

"Ah, I see." Jason reached across the table and finished cleaning Naomi's face. "Well, are you ready to go?"

"Yay! The party, the party!" Naomi squealed.

Why can't Maggie be here to share this? Jason wondered as the familiar dagger pierced his heart.

* * *

The Blazer's tires crunched on the driveway, and Jason had barely stopped the SUV before Naomi bounded out of the door and into the Burg's house. Jason shook his head and followed Naomi. Mrs. Burg stood at the door.

"Hi, Helen. How's it going?" Jason looked into the house at the herd of girls in the living room.

"Good for now, but talk to me tomorrow." Helen pulled her graying hair into a ponytail.

"I'm not sure I'll want to," Jason said, feigning disgust. "Speaking of tomorrow, what time would you like me to come get Naomi?"

Helen thought for a moment and said, "Well, any time you're ready to get her. I have breakfast and lunch planned and I can entertain the girls for quite a while, so don't worry."

"Well, how does two sound?"

"Perfect." She turned and looked toward the living room. "Well, I'm going to go supervise. I'll tell Naomi you're leaving."

"Thanks, Helen."

"Naomi, your dad's leaving!" Helen called.

Naomi streaked out of the living room.

"Bye, Daddy!" She gave Jason a kiss on his stubbly cheek as she hugged him. "Love you!"

"Love you, too! Have fun!" he called after her.

* * *

The clock on the Blazer's dash showed five thirty. Jason swerved into his driveway and parked in front of his house. He shut off the engine and sat reflecting, taking in the sight of the rose bushes and shrubbery he and Maggie had planted together. Though he smiled, the familiar ache of loss and loneliness knotted his stomach. Throughout his journey home he

The Surprise

kept telling himself how nice it would be to have an evening alone without responsibility. The hollow throb in his gut seemed to suggest otherwise.

Jason's thoughts wandered. Things had gone well with Maggie at one time; they'd often shared relaxing evenings together; watched movies or TV on the couch, laughed and enjoyed each other's company.

He rubbed his palms over his face and sighed, a familiar occurrence these days.

Where had it all gone wrong? How did I not see the end coming? Hell, how come I didn't even see the start of the end?

Thoughts of Maggie's drug use filtered into Jason's mind. He gripped the steering wheel and clenched his teeth together. His brow furrowed, and the desperation that filled his thoughts so often grew like a weed.

We'd only been married a couple of years and she started abusing. Did I do something to cause it? Wasn't I giving her what she needed?

Methamphetamines; she'd progressed from the lighter drugs to those. Where she'd got them from, Jason could only guess. The day she'd discovered the pregnancy seemed to be a turning point for Maggie.

Being pregnant brought her back to reality...

The drug use stopped, or so she said, and things returned to normal. Jason smiled and recalled how he'd got involved in every aspect of the pregnancy and fell in love with Maggie all over again.

Three years passed; three years of good married life. Jason had vowed he wouldn't ignore the signs of Maggie's drug use if they reappeared and he kept to his word. The changes, though small at first, crept into their life. Maggie didn't seem so on top of household chores; things around the house began to slip. Dishes piled up in and around the sink. The vacuum never came out of the closet; crumbs, dust and debris remained on the once clean carpet, made themselves at home there, latching onto Jason's bare feet for a vacation.

Yes, he spotted the signs all right. How could he not? Weren't they glaringly obvious this time around, more so now that they had a child in the picture? Naomi's clothing piled up in front of the washer, forever stained. Maggie used to wash them quickly, as soon as Naomi spilled something, but not anymore.

It must have been me. My fault. Maybe I didn't help enough with Naomi, and the combined stress of taking care of the house and a toddler was too much for Maggie.

In addition to the forty or more hours he put in at work, Jason thought back to how he'd shouldered more of the responsibilities at home. Recalled how he wanted to be the best husband and father he could be. Wasn't that natural? It seemed so to him, what with being the main supporter.

My fault Maggie got stressed...

Jason looked at himself in the rearview mirror; saw how his features had changed over the years. Small bags had formed under his brown eyes. Wrinkles, wrinkles of worry that Maggie had put there mocked him from the skin beside his mouth, the worry lines deeper in his brow. He stifled a sigh (sick to death of hearing himself do that) and continued to rip himself apart with thoughts of the past.

It transformed into a serious addiction. Regardless of Jason's efforts, Maggie remained steeped in her drug problems. Reality merged with fantasy, and thoughts that had been swirling inside Maggie's mind spilled into their life.

"You're having an affair with Jill, aren't you?" Maggie spat.

Jason, stunned, had been momentarily at a loss for words.

Maggie's face contorted into a mask of disdain. Jason remembered looking at her once shiny, clean hair, noticing how it had grown lackluster. It hung limply, an unwashed mess.

Maggie sneered and placed her hands on her bony hips. "What are you staring at, huh? Comparing me to *Jill*? Yeah, I know all about the pair of you!"

"What the hell are you talking about, Maggie?" Panic fluttered in Jason's chest. "I'm dedicated to you and Naomi. I'd never do anything to jeopardize the life I have. Hell, I'm trying to make us all right again, you know? Help you through this...this...rough patch..."

"Rough patch?" Maggie laughed, the sound so harsh and hollow that it frightened Jason a little.

Man, I wondered then if she'd actually lost it. Gone insane. Why didn't she take my help? How could she have thrown it all away?

With her blue eyes blazing, grinning a humorless grin, she snatched up the fireplace poker. "I'll fix you and show *you* a rough patch!"

Christ, I thought she was going to come after me with that thing!

The Blazer caught the brunt of Maggie's anger.

The neighbors called the cops, but she'd gotten me good before they got here.

His hand went to his face where Maggie punched him that night.

It was all I could do to convince the officer I didn't want to press charges, that Maggie just needed rehab.

Jason clenched his hands and pounded the steering wheel.

Divorce was the only way! After that I couldn't trust her, and getting Naomi was for Naomi's safety, not my personal agenda!

The Surprise

Rubbing his hands over his stubbly cheeks, Jason chided himself. *Damn it! Things will never get better this way. Go in, relax. What's done is done, right or wrong.*

He walked into the house. A twinge of unease unfurled in his gut. *Don't be an idiot. You're just feeling the fallout from the last two months and this is the first real time alone you've had.*

Determined to relax, Jason headed to the kitchen to decide what would be an easy dinner. *Ah look at that! Pizza, and there's Bud Light in the fridge. I can put the pizza in the oven while I take a shower.* Jason rubbed his hands together. *When I'm done I'll have beer and pizza in front of the tube. I haven't done that in forever.*

He set the oven to preheat, walked into the living room, and flipped on the TV. The local news usually spouted a bunch of unimportant garbage, but once in a while something worth watching came on.

"This is Kevin Marsh bringing you breaking news. We have just received a report of three female elopements from New Beginnings, our local mental hospital. As of yet, we have no further information, but residents are asked to be on the lookout and report any suspicious activity to the authorities. We will keep you posted as we obtain more information."

"In other news..."

Jason silenced Kevin.

Maggie's going through rehab at New Beginnings...

Jason returned to the kitchen and unwrapped the Totino's Meat Combo pizza. His mind spun. *Surely Maggie isn't one of the elopements. They keep the rehab side of the hospital under close surveillance. Besides, they'd have contacted me by now, surely?*

He slid the pizza into the oven (no pan, he liked the extra crispy crust) and thought, *Don't be silly. She's working on turning her life around.* He set the timer and took it with him so that he could hear it when it rang.

Though small, the house was comfortable. Leaving the kitchen at the back of the house, Jason walked through the living and dining room—one big room separated by a small fireplace. He padded across the short hallway to the right of the living room where the bathroom and two bedrooms were located, planning to enter the master bedroom on the left. Jason passed Naomi's bedroom to the right of the hallway and saw Mr. Bits, Naomi's cat, lying on her bed. Jason started to enter his room but stopped short. The door stood open.

I know Naomi's door was left open, but I thought I closed mine this morning before I left the house. That damn cat likes to destroy my pillows if I don't. Well, at least it looks like he left them alone today.

Jason placed the timer on his dresser and stripped down. He picked up the timer and headed to the bathroom, placing it on the edge of the sink. He started the shower and adjusted the temperature until steam poured from behind the curtain. Making sure the bathroom door stood ajar (hoping to disperse some of the heat, thus keeping steam off the mirror) he stepped under the hot shower spray, feeling some of the stress and anxiety wash away. After he finished washing he turned the water as hot as he could stand it and let the heat relax his muscles.

This is what you needed. No reason to jump at shadows.

A clatter sounded from one of the other rooms.

That cat! I didn't chase him off before I came in here. I'm sure he's on my dresser again. Jason sighed. *If it weren't for Naomi, that cat would be history...*

Jason turned off the water, dried off, and wrapped a towel around his waist. He couldn't shave yet; despite his efforts, the mirror had still fogged up. He looked at the timer and saw that it was about time for the pizza to be done.

Forget shaving tonight. Who do I need to impress? I'll just stop by my bedroom, put on some deodorant and then get the pizza out of the oven. After that I'll come back and get some boxers and maybe a pair of sweatpants if I'm too chilly.

He headed into the bedroom and glanced at his dresser. Most of the things he kept there had been knocked askew. He walked over to straighten them up and jumped; the timer went off, sending him out of his room to rescue his pizza from ruination.

Whistling, he entered the living room.

Maggie sat in his favorite armchair.

* * *

Sitting in Jason's armchair, Maggie thought about how things had fallen apart.

I just need answers. Why didn't he notice my problems sooner, or try to help? I was only looking to have a good time... Seemed in control at first...

The drugs soon controlled Maggie and it scared her.

He must have been so angry. The perfect family. That's all he ever talked about.

Maggie had fantasized about a touching moment when Jason recognized her problems, but in her mind that moment never came.

The Surprise

But Naomi came. My redemption...

Maggie smiled. Her brow furrowed, another thought marring her moment of happy recollection.

But then he had no time for me. I, I was just looking for an escape...

The drugs again, and with them came a certainty that Jason and Jill were having an affair.

I had to confront him, keep him from her. That no-good bastard took everything from me when I was most vulnerable, but I'll have my answers...

Maggie heard the timer go off and waited for Jason to discover her. The satisfaction she sought didn't materialize—Jason jerked slightly, but otherwise appeared composed, as if he'd expected her all along.

"I would have thought you would be a bit more surprised, Jason. Aren't you glad to see me?" Maggie asked. She narrowed her blue eyes.

"Well, you did make the news. What do you want, Maggie?"

"What the fuck do you *think* I want? I want some goddamn answers, Jason," she spat. "I want to know why I wasn't good enough to love, why it was so easy to take everything from me."

Look at him standing there acting like it's nothing that I'm sitting here, acting as though he has the upper hand. Huh, and wearing nothing but a towel. He's probably showered to get ready to see her... I thought I'd botched those plans...

"What do you want me to say, Maggie?" Jason shrugged his shoulders. "No matter what I tell you, you won't believe it unless it's what you expect to hear."

Anger awoke in Maggie, flaring like campfire coals in a breeze. "That's a load of bullshit and you know it! You stand there and act like it wasn't your fault that I was stuck in that godforsaken detox place. Then on top of it, you leave me when I need you the most and you take my daughter from me."

He's so fucking indifferent I just want to choke the life out of him!

The harder she suppressed the desire, the longer she looked at him, the more her anger felt like a wave, starting small at first, but building into a catastrophic tsunami.

"Maggie, it wasn't my sole decision to send you to detox. Besides it was—"

"For my own good. Everyone feeds me that bullshit cliché. That's not even the main reason I'm here, Jason. Tell me why you left and took my daughter!"

"Do *you* want to hear that I couldn't take it anymore, that I thought you were a shitty mother?" Jason began pacing back and forth. He rubbed his flattop. "Fine, I'll admit you were a wreck. It *is* true that I couldn't take it anymore. Look at my Blazer, for Christ's sake!" Jason pointed out of the window with a shaky hand. "Did you really believe that after that I would trust you with our daughter?"

She heard anger creeping into his voice. *Good, if he's pissed enough, maybe he'll admit to it all. Not just that he'd had enough, but also admit that he was screwing Jill the whole time...*

* * *

This is ridiculous. I'm here in a towel arguing with my escapee ex-wife and I'm pissed besides. I need to keep calm, because both of us losing it is going to be a disaster. Maggie always could push my buttons.

"And the tart on the side had absolutely nothing to do with it I suppose?" said Maggie. "Oh wait, I forgot. You keep trying to bullshit me that you never slept with her. I don't suppose you're willing to admit it yet?" Maggie pointed at Jason. "You! You don't have the balls, or did you manage to grow a set while I was away?"

"For fuck's sake! Jill has nothing to do with this!"

Maggie launched herself from the chair, her hands out in front of her, and moved straight for Jason's throat. Sidestepping just in time, he watched Maggie sprawl onto the floor. She stood up, her face red.

Shit! It's gone too far...

"Why, goddamn it? WHY??" she shrieked.

Reluctant to turn his back to her, Jason's mind sought to form an escape route while keeping her in sight. Which room should he go to?

Maggie snarled and pounced at him like a rabid lioness. Not quick enough to fully evade her this time, they both fell to the floor. Jason's left hip hit the edge of the coffee table. Maggie landed half on top of him, and Jason used the momentum to roll them one more half turn so that he was on top of her.

"Just stop for a minute and listen, Maggie. This is stupid. If you want to talk, fine, but we need to calm down."

Maggie appeared not to have heard him, or maybe just didn't care about what he had to say. She reached under the towel he wore and grabbed hold of his balls. Pain drove all other thoughts from Jason's mind. Maggie twisted his testicles; a grin of malice spread across her face. Jason lost his leverage on her. With one more vicious wrench, Maggie let go. Jason rolled onto his side, clutching his throbbing groin.

Maggie leapt to her feet with amazing agility, and Jason didn't much

The Surprise

care for the way she glared down at him

"Just...wait...listen..." Jason gasped. Beads of sweat sprung out on his forehead, and he felt some trickle down his temple. "Things are getting out of hand. We need to..."

Maggie landed a well-placed kick to his kidney. "Don't you tell me I need to calm down! You have no idea how much pain you've caused me, and now it's *my* turn!"

Jason saw Maggie pull her leg back, aiming for his kidney again. Jason scrambled out of the way. Her foot landed on his rump instead, causing his face to rake across the carpet. Maggie moved to come after him again. The phone rang, its shrill sound seeming to rend the air.

"Are you missing your date?" she hissed.

Jesus, I wish she would go back to yelling. Maybe she'd attract some attention, get someone to call the cops. Plus, she seems more normal when she's yelling.

Somehow her silence was far more threatening, a spider waiting for its prey to make the fatal mistake. He didn't want to hurt her, but on the other hand, he much preferred to keep most of his body parts intact and undamaged. Jason hunched next to the chair trying to decide what he should do.

Maybe I should offer her a beer and tell her I'll share my pizza. That thought almost made him laugh and he wondered about his sanity. *For God's sake don't laugh. You'll cause her to really lose it.* Two realizations came to him. First, the phone had stopped ringing, so someone might come to see if he was alright. Second, the pizza was still in the oven. Surely that meant it would start burning soon.

A smoking pizza might be enough of a distraction for me to get away from Maggie and call the cops. I don't want to hurt her. There has to be somewhere to go, something to do...

***

Her whole life had been unfair, and the man she loved with all her heart didn't love her anymore. She could tell by the way he was looking up at her. Disgusted with herself, Maggie still couldn't repress the desire to tear into Jason and beat him to a bloody pulp. Her heart, beyond broken, or even shattered, literally ached. It felt as though she had no heart left and the one responsible for that feeling was cowering in front of her like a rabbit cornered by a fox.

The two halves of Maggie's mind kept arguing back and forth.

Apologize, leave, and hope for the best, Maggie...
Make him pay for all the hurt he's caused, Maggie...
A difficult decision; both sides relied on the same idea: no matter what happened or what she did, it was surely over between her and Jason. If that was true, then what was the answer?
Leave, Maggie... Let him go on living and hope that even though you can never be together, you might get a shot at joint custody for Naomi... Yes, you need to leave, turn yourself in, and hope for the best...
No! NO! You can't allow him to get away with everything he's done to you! How can you trust you'll ever get joint custody after the spineless bastard has taken all you love while your back was turned?
Maggie knew she had to listen to one of the voices. Just one.
I'll wait for a sign showing me what to do, who to heed...
She looked over at the fireplace. Saw the poker. And understood.

* * *

Jason watched the different masks of emotions flit over Maggie's face. She seemed in a world of her own making and never looked directly at him. His gaze swept the room for anything he might be able to defend himself with. He recognized the signs—the look—that she was about to flip.
I may actually have to hurt her to save myself.
Jason's stomach knotted at the thought. She was further gone than he had first realized, her facial expressions were evidence of that. Jason noticed the candle on the end table next to the chair. A big Wal-Mart candle that came in its own glass container. Jason figured it to be about the size of a small coffee can. He slowly edged closer to the table, his gaze trained on Maggie, whose own gaze turned to the fire poker.
Maggie raced for it. Jason dove for the candle. Knowing that the candle wouldn't be a very effective tool against the fire poker, Jason sacrificed some power for aim and heaved the candle at Maggie. It struck her left hip, and she cried out in pain and surprise. Jason jumped up to rush at her. He came in low to tackle her around the waist, but Maggie recovered and raised the poker over her head. She brought it flat side down on Jason's back. He let out a yelp that sounded more like a dog than a man, and threw himself forward. His body connected with Maggie's, and she crashed down onto the fireplace tools. She hit the ground and dropped the poker. Jason scrambled to his feet to get it out of her reach. A sharp pain shot across his back with his movement.
Please, God. Give me lightning speed, not the speed of an overturned

The Surprise

tortoise! Jeez...

Maggie seized the poker again and a maniacal laugh erupted from her mouth. Jason grabbed the shovel from the tool set and blocked an arcing blow from Maggie's weapon. Like a batter swinging for a home run, he brought the shovel around, catching Maggie across the left knee. Maggie screamed in pain and dropped to the ground. Jason struck her arm the held the poker until she lost her grip on it. Quickly moving out of her reach, he grabbed the poker. Maggie snarled and lunged at him; raked her blunt nails across his chest and managed to draw blood. Jason felt like someone had poured small lines of lighter fluid on his chest and lit a match to them. Maggie let a right hook fly, popping him in the eye. The unexpected punch rocked his head back, and pain blossomed behind his eye. Maggie leapt on top of him and placed her hands around his neck. She squeezed.

"Jesus Christ, Maggie! Stop!" Jason wheezed. He worked to get his weight shifted to throw her off his chest.

Obviously no longer listening, Maggie made a terrifying guttural sound like a wild animal.

Jason rocked and managed to throw her off his chest toward the fireplace. Careful not to straddle her again, he pinned down her shoulders. Maggie reached into the fireplace, grabbed a chunk of wood, and attempted to rearrange Jason's skull structure on the left side of his head. The wood tore his scalp—Jason felt hot blood seep from the wound—and absurdly realized his head sounded hollow. His vision blurred, began to narrow, and he fought to keep from losing consciousness.

Got to keep awake. She'll kill me for sure if I black out...How can I... I need to get her...away...from me...I need to...uh...

His thoughts fuzzed along the edges. He felt the log *thwump* him once more, this time across his right shoulder. He turned to Maggie and watched as she dragged the log back towards her. His flesh turned to hamburger.

She's...pulling out...all the stops...now, God...help me.

Maggie lifted the log above her head and brought it back down again and again on Jason's back. He curled into a ball, terrified of the grunting noises she made.

Oh...God...someone...help...me...

* * *

I finally have the bastard right where I want him.

Maggie paid no mind to the pain in her knee and arm where Jason had hit her. One goal consumed Maggie—to make him pay.

He's the one at fault for my pain and problems. I'll fucking show him the kind of pain he showed me.

Looking down on him as she brought the log down again and again she felt a sick kind of glee at his helplessness. She finally had her opportunity to pay him back and she was using it to her full benefit.

Jason's paying, Maggie…
Yes! I'm finally making Jason pay.
Maggie?
What?
Isn't that someone at the door?
Who cares? They can't help him, I'm making him pay.
A crash sounded.
Someone's in the house, Maggie…
Shut up! It doesn't matter because Jason's paying…

Two hands gripped Maggie from behind and tried to pull her away from Jason. *Then* it mattered. She turned to see a male police officer. Anger at her attack being thwarted surged through her blood, and she smacked the officer on the side of the face with the log.

Another officer raced in, tackled Maggie before she could resist.

* * *

Sitting at the kitchen table in his boxers, having an EMT check his injuries, the whole evening seemed surreal to Jason. He knew Maggie had gained entrance in by using the spare key he kept on top of the porch light fixture.

I knew I should have moved that key, but Maggie was in rehab. I guess I thought there wasn't a rush. Jason rubbed his eyes, wincing at the pain where Maggie had punched him. *Thank God the neighbors called the police.*

"Well, man, you're good to go. You just have some cuts and bruises, and you'll probably have one killer of a headache once that Advil wears off, but you'll be fine," the EMT said as he packed his things to leave.

"Good to know. Thanks." Jason looked up at the EMT and gave him a weak smile. *I bet I'll be stiff tomorrow too. Jesus, I hope Maggie isn't any worse off that I am.*

"Your, uh, wife, is it? She's outside being checked over." The EMT glanced out of the window. "And it looks like she'll be taken away; cops are with her," said the EMT.

"Yeah, I guess she will."

The Surprise

Jason had been angry and scared, but sitting in the kitchen, sadness and pity replaced his former emotions. Guilt soured the bile in his gut; not for what he had done to Maggie during their confrontation, but for Jill, who sat across from him in his kitchen now. She'd been the caller while he and Maggie had wrestled on the floor.

"I have to admit something to you," Jill said. She studied her manicured nails. "I...I had planned on calling you before I heard about the elopements from the rehab place." She looked into Jason's eyes. "I guess lately I've had more than a friendly interest in you."

Jason shifted in his chair, but his brown gaze never left Jill's blue one. "You know I didn't realize it until now, but I feel the same about you."

Maybe that's where the guilt is coming from. Even so, I can see myself with Jill when the dust settles. Jason rubbed his head and winced. *It's not in spite of Maggie; I'm not wrong wanting Jill. I guess even if it is, it's the way I feel.*

Jason sighed, got up, and gave Jill a hug. It would all work out somehow.

The Sickness
by
Amanda Tieman

I guess I have always been good at hiding things that are wrong. I push emotions (which to me have always been too messy) down into this place where I don't have to deal with them. Easier that way. That's how I've been dealing with the problem I have now.

There isn't much you need to know about me that you won't find out when I tell my sordid tale, but I'll tell you a little, so you can understand where I'm coming from. I'm a twenty-six year old woman living in BFE, Wyoming, with Xander, my quirky Great Dane. I also have a small circle of friends consisting of one guy I've known since high school (who also lives here) and an ex-roommate from college who lives in North Dakota.

Now that I think of it, you may not even be able to call that a circle. You may think it pathetic, and I wouldn't begrudge you that opinion, but I find it to be much more manageable that way. I like my privacy and, looking back, it's a damn good thing. Anyhow, I will warn you, my tale is rather graphic and I advise those who prefer smiley faces, hearts, flowers, and warm fuzzy feelings to find something else to read. Just a thought...

It never ceases to amaze me how a trip can go from great to shit with no forewarning. That's how the camping trip went. Spring fever gripped me, and I happen to be an avid camper. I craved to go adventuring with Xander. While camping, we both get the chance to unwind and run around like the nuts we are. It also gives me time to get a fresh perspective on my life. One weekend in March looked great for such a trip (unseasonably nice weather), so Saturday morning I packed everything in the truck, and we headed out to the lake. I left the passenger side window down as we cruised through the hills. Xander kept his head out the window, his jowls and tongue flapping in the wind. Occasionally, he bit at the air which produced a whooshing sound. I patted his side and smiled.

Early spring camping in Wyoming is great. It's totally solitary as opposed summer when you have less space at your camp site than in your yard. Plus, the parks don't charge for camping early in the season.

The trip started off fantastic. Xander swam in the lake... Okay, maybe *swam* is too grand a description. He usually wades out up to his knees, but got excited and ended up in deeper water. In his panic, Xander tried to jump over the water instead of swimming. Seeing a one hundred sixty pound dog trying to jump over water is quite the sight. Just imagine a springboard under the water that launches him back out every time he lands. I found it

The Sickness

rather amusing.

Once he safely returned to shore, Xander and I hiked around the lake on some of the deer paths, working up an appetite. We climbed over rocky outcroppings to look out over the lake. The setting sun glinted off the lake's surface. The sky, a fiery orange with wisps of pink, reminded me of cotton candy strung across the horizon. A faint breeze laced with the scent of sage ruffled my hair. After enjoying the view for a few minutes we headed back to camp.

I placed Xander's blanket next to the fire and roasted some cheddar bratwursts. Xander relaxed while I munched and watched the stars come out. The harvest moon shimmered over the lake. So far, a wonderful trip.

Coyotes yipped in the distance.

Those coyotes sound odd. Their voices are deeper than normal.

Xander began to pace around camp, and I noticed the coyotes sounded as though they were getting closer.

"Xander, come here!" I called. He sat next to me, and I stroked his head for a while. Xander went around the other side of the fire and lay down on his blanket. Before long he was snoring, and I had forgotten about the coyotes.

From under drooping eyelids, I looked across the dying embers and watched Xander's slumbering black form melt into the darkness. A loud crack caused me to sit bolt upright. I held my breath wondering what might be hiding in the darkness.

It's a deer or an antelope...

A guttural growl issued from the shadows.

So much for the idea of a cuddly critter. That thing sounds huge...

I reached for my Beretta that I always keep with me when I go out camping. Xander still snoozed away. He seemed unfazed, but I was on edge.

I don't like shooting animals, but I'm not about to become a chew toy for some unknown beast because of my affinity for animals.

Eyes shone in the dark. I took aim, but too late. A beast lunged at me, all gleaming teeth. Saliva flew from its grotesque, glistening chops. With the same wiry and brownish tan fur as a coyote, it stood nearly twice the size of Xander. I didn't expect the thing to attack with such ferocity, and my shot went off into the trees. The thing pinned me on the ground—it snarled and snapped at any part of my body that it could get its mouth near. Claws dug into my shoulders, and the beast bit my forearm. Pain exploded. Searing heat flowed from the bite wound and blossomed in my chest. The beast's strength, so strong, began to overpower me. I was losing the battle.

My God I'm going to be eaten by the biggest coyote I've ever seen! Jesus, it's like the damn thing is venomous. Impossible...

The commotion woke Xander and he was on the thing instantly. He jumped on the creature's back and worked to get at its throat. The thing thrashed, moving farther from me, and attempted to buck Xander. The beast screamed, sounding more human than animal, and threw Xander to the ground.

"Xander, here!"

As soon as he was clear I emptied the rest of my clip (sixteen shots) at the thing. I know some of the shots hit home; the thing roared and glared in my direction.

I thought I was a better shot than that. It's bleeding and pissed, but still alive...

It looked back and forth between Xander and me; seemed to decide it was outnumbered. It loped off into the darkness through a thicket. Xander chased after the beast to the edge of the tree-line, then came back. I petted him. "Good boy, Xander."

I checked him for injuries. Luckily, he was unharmed. I staggered to the truck on shaky legs, got my first aid kit, and began to examine the extent of my damage. Neither the claw marks nor the bite were extremely deep; not as bad as I'd expected. I cleaned and dressed the wounds. My nerves hummed. I jumped at the smallest sounds and stared at every shadow with suspicion.

Just haul ass and get everything packed up. You can decide where to go and what to do from there. Hospital probably.

I took down the tent with shaking hands and threw everything in the back of the truck willy-nilly. I made a quick check to see if anything would blow out while driving. It all looked good. Xander and I got into the truck, headed for town at top speed. During the thirty-five mile trip, Xander periodically nudged my arm with his nose and whined. I tried to soothe him, but he remained uneasy.

By the time we pulled up in front of the house I rent, all the adrenaline had run through my system. Bone tired, I led Xander into the house and collapsed on the couch. I fell asleep almost immediately.

* * *

I'm pinned under the stinking foul beast that tore open my arm, but this time Xander's nowhere to be found. I scream as the creature drives me to the ground. It tears open my throat; blood spurts from my neck and the

The Sickness

(coyote?) thing slurps it up. Finally, it rips open my chest, and I actually feel the heat as my chest gapes and the creature devours my heart...

I'm not dead. I'm loping along on all fours, chasing a rabbit. I close the distance and leap. It squeals in terror. Without hesitation, I bite its head off and guzzle the warm coppery fluid that pours from what's left of its neck. Once the flow has stopped, I rip open the rabbit with my claws and consume its heart in one gulp. My hunger still rages, and I chase down an antelope, repeating my actions with the rabbit.

I woke up. Sat up. Sweat ran between my shoulder blades. I swung my legs off the couch and winced at the cramp in my neck.

Stupid. What was I thinking sleeping on the couch? My arms feel like bricks.

Xander danced the potty dance. I stood up and padded through the kitchen to let him into the back yard. My ghostly refection stared back at me from the glass in the screen door. My short blonde hair stuck up every which way, and bags had begun to form under my blue eyes.

Good God! I look like shit. I'm not in such bad shape that I can't jump in the shower quick before going to the hospital.

I undressed to get in the shower and un-bandaged my arm, quite surprised to find that my wounds were not anywhere near as bad as they seemed the night before. Both the teeth and claw marks were hardly more than scratches.

Guess I don't need stitches after all. Good. I'm not spending the rest of my day waiting for some eeijit doctor to violate my arm and charge me more than a month's pay to do it.

I stepped in the shower and hissed as the water hit the claw marks on my shoulder. It only stung for a moment, then the hot water sluiced away the aches and pains from the previous night. I stood in the shower after I finished washing, enjoying the smells of my Herbal Essences shampoo and my white tea and ginger body wash.

I stepped out of the shower, dried off, and wrapped myself in the towel. I combed my hair, brushed my teeth, then went around the corner into my room to get dressed. I put on a blue tank top and sweatpants. I re-bandaged my arm and put away my camping gear. I'd had my fill of camping for a while.

I plopped down on the couch and turned on *Elizabethtown* (yeah, I'm an Orlando Bloom sucker), and Xander lay on the couch next to me, snoring away. I'd barely got through the first thirty minutes and my stomach began to roar.

Man, I am hungry...

I paused my movie, padded into the kitchen, and rummaged through the fridge. I found a pound of hamburger I'd saved as a treat for Xander. Tearing open the package I devoured it raw while standing at the counter. My hunger sharpened. I pulled packages of meat from the freezer—two steaks, a package of four chicken breasts, four pork chops, and another pound of hamburger—and gnawed them until they thawed enough for me to eat them with ease.

What in the hell is wrong with me?

After I had exhausted the supply of meat, I looked down and saw Xander lying at my feet. He looked up at me and whined.

So it's not just me...

I walked over to the sink, washed my hands and face, and shoved the packages from the meat down into the garbage and buried them. Every time I looked at them, I got an icy feeling in my gut.

I filled Xander's bowl with his kibble, headed back to the living room, and started the movie up again.

Jesus Christ! Xander must have stepped on the remote...

Sound blasted from the speakers. I snatched up the remote and turned down the volume. The sound remained at the same level.

Great. The frockin' TV is broken.

The indicator on the screen showed the volume at a normal level, yet my ears told me different. I turned off the TV. My mind raced, but all I wanted to do was escape, so I decided to read.

I picked up *It* by Stephen King. I've read that book so many times, but it's still one of my favorites. It didn't take long before the words totally absorbed me. I'm not really sure how long I'd been reading when my stomach rumbled again, bringing me back to reality. I smelled one of the neighbors barbecuing.

If I want any dinner I'd better go get some groceries. I ate all the damn meat.

I gathered my keys, my wallet (I don't carry a purse, I always leave them sitting somewhere), whistled for Xander to follow, and drove to the grocery store. Funny, the only sign of a cookout I noticed was smoke coming from a yard nearly four blocks away.

The trip was fairly uneventful except it took all my will power to keep from ripping into the packages of meat at the store. My shopping was rather limited; I only bought meats. I planned to barbecue.

Upon my arrival home, the meat never made it to the grill.

This is so disgusting! I should at least cook it a little.

All the reasoning in my mind couldn't convince me to take the time to cook anything I'd purchased. The desire to eat it raw was too strong to deny. Repulsed, I took out the garbage.

Physical and mental exhaustion overtook me, so I decided to hit the sack early. Xander followed me down the hall to my room and took his accustomed place on the bed. He watched me as I changed into my version of pajamas—a sports bra and boxers. I climbed into bed and was asleep almost before my head hit the pillow.

* * *

I woke up feeling rather relaxed. The nightmares from the previous night didn't haunt my sleep. I lay there with my eyes closed and realized my pajamas were wet. I opened my eyes, saw Xander, and shrieked.

A barely recognizable Xander lay in the corner of my room. Xander, my pal and roommate, was a bloody mess. In my horror everything became vivid. The metallic scent of blood, the ragged edges of the gaping hole in Xander's belly and chest, the way his head was nearly torn completely away, the bite marks all over his body, the splashes of blood on the wall and carpet. Blood splattered my bed, my hands, my *body*. I ran to the bathroom and saw myself in the mirror.

Blood painted my face. Clots hung in my hair. My eyes had widened to such a degree the whites showed all around. I looked deranged, felt insanity pluck my nerves. I had to be, I'd murdered my dog in my sleep. Hadn't I?

Why? Why? WHY?? What's going on? How... Jesus, no!

My mind went round and round. Nausea clenched my stomach with greasy fingers, and I turned to the toilet and vomited. I sobbed and puked, and sobbed some more. Finished, I turned on the shower to nearly pure hot water and stepped in. My stomach churned at the sight of all the blood and bits of meat that swirled down the drain.

My Xander! Dear God, no...

Grief constricted my chest and knotted my stomach. I stood in the shower, the water scalding my skin, until I stopped crying.

I have got to do something about this, but I have to take care of Xander first.

Armed with new resolve, I stepped out of the shower, dried off, and got dressed, careful not to dirty my clothing with blood. I went in the kitchen to gather some things to take care of Xander. I found the big black garbage bags that I used to pick up the leaves in the yard, a large serrated knife, and took them back to my bedroom. The smell of carnage seemed stronger than when I'd woken up. I expected to get sick again, but the smell didn't nauseate, it enticed. My stomach growled.

No, please. I don't want to... I can't...

I managed to avoid taking bites from what was left of Xander, horrified at the way my mouth watered and my stomach grumbled as I cut dangling pieces off the remains so they would fit into bags. Those kinds of desires can drive you crazy. It only took two bags; there wasn't much left of Xander.

I wanted to bury him in the back yard where he loved to lay and sun himself, but I still had the blood in my room to clean up. Instinct screamed at me to hurry, I didn't have much time. In the end I put Xander's remains in the dumpster behind my house. It almost killed me to do that, but I didn't quite know what else to do. I couldn't very well go around telling someone that I'd eaten my dog in my sleep.

I went back in to clean up my room. As I scrubbed the carpet, I reflected on the past day and a half.

Eating all that raw meat... Poor Xander... My arm... That beast... No way. That's even crazier than anything that has been going on. I have to have some mental illness, 'cos the thought that the beast attacking me has some bearing on my current situation isn't even an option.

I wanted to believe I had a mental issue. I could have gone for help in that case, but my arm was the clincher. Mental illness does not cause wounds to heal at a prodigious rate.

Maybe I'd been bitten by a werewolf.

That was the only explanation that made any sense. That thing that bit me seemed like a coyote mostly because that was the only way my mind could explain it. The burning sensation came from the saliva as I was infected by the bite. The more I thought of it, the beast had qualities of a coyote, but didn't look much like one really; too big, and the body structure wasn't right, like it could have got up and ran on two legs, though it clearly preferred to be on four. Suffice to say, the more I thought about the whole situation, the more the explanation made sense to me.

Werewolves. Surely they're a myth, something from movies. But what if it's true? How in the hell am I supposed to deal with this? Stupid, but what the hell...

I logged on the Internet. I wasn't in the mood (and quite honestly, was a bit afraid to be around people) to go to the library. I thought I knew about werewolves before I started searching for anything that might help me. I had no idea there were so many beliefs and ideas.

What a load of crap! Wolf-skin belts? Friendly werewolves? Jesus, I guess this is where Hollywood really got it right.

I wasn't particularly thrilled with my discoveries. So far, my experiences

The Sickness

had been on a par with Hollywood's portrayal of lycanthropy.

I... Shit, what do I do?

I logged off the Internet. Up until recently I loved werewolf movies and books. At a loss for anything else to do, I broke out my collection of horror movies and stories. I didn't watch the movies all the way through, nor did I read the entire books. I went straight to the relevant parts.

Fucking filmmakers! Why can't they agree on anything?

Almost every movie had a different way to cure or (God forbid) kill a werewolf. I really wasn't any better off than when I had started my search for information. The only immediate solution I could come up with, other than killing myself (which I wasn't even sure I could do), was to get out of town. I knew if I stuck around something horrible was bound to happen.

Am I really considering this? Yeah, I guess I am. Crazy maybe, but some instinct is telling me I've been bitten by a werewolf. Let's face it; this could be a rather painful and noisy process too. I don't really need concerned neighbors calling the police.

I selected only two items of camping gear; a cooler, which I loaded with meats, and my sleeping bag. I didn't need anything else.

* * *

It seems fitting enough. This has to be the spot.

I set up camp about where Xander and I camped two nights before. I hoped the werewolf that had bitten me would come back. After all, one theory of a cure was to kill the werewolf that bit you and then eat its heart. Intuition told me that was true.

I built a fire and continued to wrestle with emotions. I felt so lost and there was no way I could go to anyone. What, was I going to get on the phone and say, "Yeah, hey, Mom. What's new with me? Oh I'm a lycanthrope... No a *lycanthrope*, you know, werewolf?" Yeah, right. I'd be in a straight jacket and a rubber room before I knew what happened.

I hiked around, ate meat from the cooler (still repulsed, but getting used to it), and thought. By the time twilight hit and I was headed back to my camp I had some idea of what I could do if I couldn't come up with a cure; I would have to avoid people.

Night fell. The blood in my veins seemed to heat up. Not metaphorically, but literally. I wondered if a fever was on its way. The night appeared to get colder even though I sat so close to the fire that the skin on my shins turned red. Then the heat took over, as though it were noon instead of eleven at night. I got up and paced around. My blood and bones itched. I know that sounds strange, but there was an itch that ran deep through my entire body. I looked up at the sky; the moon seemed so large.

I worried if I were indeed a werewolf that the whole experience of changing was going to be painful, but the itch when it first started was the worst. My whole body tingled. Not an unpleasant tingle, more like a lover caressing my body. I stripped my clothes off and stood in the moonlight, stared at the sky. I ran on pure instinct; so *sensual*.

This is like the best sex I've ever had! This is fucking incredible!

I looked at my hands as I ran, saw my fingers grow shorter and claws sprout from the ends. My knees buckled back in an origami trick and I dropped to all fours. I heard myself moaning as if in the throes of passion, the sound seeming far away. My thighs grew thicker, more sinewy and far more powerful. With shoulders widened, I thrilled at the feeling of power my new form held. An explosion of ecstasy ripped through my body, akin to the most intense orgasm I've ever had. I tilted my head back and let out a scream, vaguely aware that it sounded much more like a howl.

Transforming was the last thing I remembered.

* * *

I awoke to the sound of birds, the smell of fresh blood, and the feeling of a body against mine.

Oh, dear Jesus, please! I didn't see anyone around for at least a couple of miles when I set up camp. Let this be an animal next to me.

I opened my eyes and saw a lean, muscular guy about my age beside me. Covered in blood. He looked dead.

FUCK! Shit, what the fuck am I going to do now?

The man rolled over and opened his eyes. I screeched, my heart pounding, and scrabbled away from him.

He sat up, yawned, and rubbed his eyes. He looked at me as though I were nuts. "Are you okay?"

"I... I thought I'd, I mean, I thought you were dead." I looked into his eyes—the most amazing hazel color I'd ever seen.

He smiled.

Wow, his teeth are so white.

"You don't know what happened last night, do you?" He had a slightly amused look on his face.

"I guess not." I didn't know what else to say. The tightening of drying blood ran all over my stitch-stark naked body, yet he didn't seem to be alarmed.

The Sickness

"You seemed fresh, but I was sure you'd remember. You don't recall *anything* about last night?" His brow knitted under the shaggy mop of sandy hair covering his head.

Fresh? Wait is he a... No, no way. If I ask him he'll think I'm bonkers.

"Wait," I said. "You don't seem concerned about this situation at all. What's going on here?" I couldn't stop staring at this gorgeous man. I felt a strong attraction to him, in spite of the situation.

He laughed, deep and sexy. Lust stirred in my groin.

"You don't have to pretend you're lost. I'm a lycan just like you. Now really, what do you remember from last night?"

Blood rushed to my cheeks, heated them.

Just tell him all you remember is transforming. You don't have to describe how it felt...

"Uh all I remember is changing," I said and looked at my bloody hands before glancing back at him.

Surprise etched on his face, his eyebrows rose. "Whoa, you're telling me that's it? How long have you been a lycan?"

"I was bitten two nights ago. I think this was the first time I transformed."

He looked at me, his mouth agape.

"That fresh? You're *that* fresh? I was sure you were at least two or three months in."

"I'm sorry, I'm still confused here. One, I don't know who you are, and two, you're talking like you remember everything from last night. Don't you black out when you transform?"

"My name's Ian, and after a while you stop blacking out. How long it takes depends on the person. You have to want to control your transformation. It's a lot like meditation." He flashed me a sexy grin, and my stomach flipped. "By the way, it'd be nice to know who *you* are too."

"I'm Alex. So how long did it take you to get yours under control?"

"Something like eight months to get to where I could remember everything I did after I transformed, but I still struggle to control my actions while I'm in lycan form. It's hard. Take last night. We managed to stay away from any people, but..." His face turned red and he looked out over the lake. "Uh, we, you know..."

I stifled a giggle, not because of what he was saying, but because of the abrupt change in his demeanor. "I know where you're going." Something occurred to me. "So how long have you been a...lycan?"

"A little over a year. I was out hunting with two of my friends and we were attacked." Ian's eyes clouded. "I was the only one who survived. The authorities wrote it off as a bear attack. That's what I thought had happened at first. It was the only thing that made any sense."

"I know what you mean. I thought I was attacked by a coyote. The only reason that I made it was…" I cleared my throat, but the lump there was tenacious. My voice wavered as I said, "My dog Xander jumped on the werewolf as it attacked me and gave me a chance to shoot at it."

Ian moved closer, sat next to me, and put his arm around my shoulders. Far from being awkward, his nearness was comforting. I leaned my head on his shoulder and cried. The whole thing still seemed surreal. After I had myself under control I asked him, "Is there any cure? Have you looked?"

Ian shook his head. "Not that I've been able to find. Other than dying, the best thing I could come up with was to get as much control over it as I could. Some days it works better than others. I haven't stopped looking, but I'm getting less and less hopeful."

I sighed. "Will you help me? Control it, I mean."

He favored me with that smile again. "I suppose I could be persuaded to do that." He leaned over and kissed me. I'd like to say his action surprised me, but I'd been hoping for it the whole time.

* * *

It's been almost two years since that morning. Ian and I are still together. He's helped me control myself in lycan form and I've been helping him too. Every full moon we take ourselves as far from people as we can and chase antelope and deer and eat our fill.

It's been surprisingly easy to hide my new life from my friends and family. They already know I'm an avid camper. Ian and I told the truth in so much as we admitted to meeting on a camping trip. We just tell everyone we like to go camping, just the two of us, once a month. We tell them it's to celebrate how we first met. It sounds cheesy to me, but they buy it.

We're starting to think being lycans isn't such a bad thing. We haven't hurt anyone since we started helping each other, though the possibility is always there. We've spent many nights discussing options for our future and decided we don't need a cure. Being in lycan form is scary, but it's also the most incredible experience I've ever had. Sensations are more intense, and life is simpler, at least to some degree. We're happy and we're taking control of our situations as best we can.

Having told my little tale, I leave you with just one warning: be careful when you go camping, at least in Wyoming. Stay closer to groups of people—you'll be better off…

Biography

Amanda Tieman is an aspiring author. She graduated from the University of Wyoming in 2004 with a B.A. in Spanish Education and a B.A. in Psychology. Amanda lives in Casper with her Great Dane, Ansel, and her parakeet, Persephone.

An excerpt from
Decimate
A Horror Anthology

Lourella's Kin

by

Ian Rochford

Available at Wild Child Publishing.com

Ian Rochford

No doubt about it, the swamp surely has changed since Lourella passed over. We buried her, with a singing out, at midnight during the last transit of Sirius, wrapped only in the old length of silver-flecked cloth that she said was her birthing gown, as was her wishes. That cloth wasn't made of anything I'd ever seen before, and it seemed to wrap itself around her old body as soon as it touched it. She said it had belonged to her father—that it was royal cloth.

She was Mama's grandmama, oldest of our clan, and she told us her passing would see a change come down. No one really knew what she was on about, but they seemed sure we'd all be leaving the swamp and going into town maybe. Us young 'uns, we didn't feel so good about that—the town folk, they didn't like us much. They called us hicks and inbreeders, though they were always happy to trade stuff for our croc skins, and they paid good money for Lemuel's flackweed, dried an' chopped. I can't smoke it, just makes me sick, but the townies loved it.

Mama's own Mama, who was Lourella's daughter Syrena, had already passed over herself more than a hound's age ago, but she would have liked Lourella's sending off. We baked her favourite Gnarlroot bread, and Lemuel brewed a batch of Flackweed Whisky. I was allowed to join in with the elders, but I didn't see the whole night through. I got skunk rotten on the Flackweed brew, which is real sweet and easy to drink, and I passed out in Lemuel's coracle.

A short time after Lourella's burying, the change started coming over the swamp. It got warmer first, and the ground grew darker. It began to get firmer and sort of moist. Well, moist in a different way, like it was sweaty, and it smelled different, too. Like the smell when Lemuel was skinning crocs. Then, other things started changing. Little Mazy, she was the first one to notice that the trees were different.

"They's wavin' to me as I poled by," she told Mama. "Real friendly like, an' I swears one of them sang, too."

Mama looked at her, real level. "Trees don't sing, child, an' they was probably just a-wavin' in the wind."

Mazy just said, "Yes, Mama," and winked at me as she went to do her chores.

Mama knew, like all of us, that there hadn't been any wind in the swamp for days—the air was sitting heavy with vapours, and we could sort of see eddies swirl in the steam. That croc-smell was stronger, too, and most of the birds had left the swamp. Mama wasn't scared, but she knew something was changing, and I think she had some idea what was coming. We all knew the swamp was different, could feel it, like. Hell, by the end of the first

Lourella's Kin

week, we were changing, too.

My hands, they were a lot tougher. I could let the ol' hemp punt cable slide through my palms now, and it wouldn't burn. They were getting like leather. Like Lourella's hands used to be. They was tough. I remember she used to chop up croc eggs on her bare palm with Gramps' ol' straight razor. It weren't sharp as it used to be, but it was a long way from dull. An' they were starting to get scaly on the backs, just like Lourella's.

Mama didn't say much. She knew way more than she was saying, that's what I thought. She and Lemuel used to sit out on the porch at night, laughing and talking about how the townies were gonna get the surprise of their lives.

"Yeah," said Lemuel, cackling an' a-shakin' in his chair, "Gonna be the last one they get too, I reckon!" Something in the way he said it made me feel warm and hungry.

Lourella used to sit out back on the porch by the water, looking up at the stars with those funny yellow eyes of hers. She'd point up at the bright one she called Sirius, and she'd say to me, "That's it, boy. That's where we come from. Ma home, an' where the seed for all ma kin come from."

She had this story about her father. His name was Ghol Dh'ralla Barakyl—isn't that a mouthful? Anyway, she said that old Ghol had come down from Sirius, way back before there was cars and stuff, and that he had mated with an Earth woman named Drusilla, who died giving birth to Lourella. When I asked what had happened to Drusilla, she looked at me real solemn and said, "Why, Ghol ate her, of course. It was his mark or respect an' grief, child."

Then it was that I understood why we always ate our dead, though we were never allowed to tell anyone about that.

"Sure is, Lem. But that'll change soon. One day, I'm gonna make this place just like old Ghol's home." She turned her pale, scaly old face to me and grinned with those wicked teeth. "It's the way of things, boy, just you see. That's why when I die, your Mama an' Lemuel are gonna bury me in the swamp instead of eatin' me. Shit, Lemuel, reckon I'd be too tough to chew on anyways, eh?" She broke off, laughing and coughing. Lemuel was laughing right along with her. "Sure," she went on when she had settled down. "When ol' Lourella goes into the ground, everythin' gonna change."

Well, she was right. Nothing's the same anymore. I went down to her grave, and even the ground itself wasn't like soil. It was more like quivering red meat; it moved and pulsed with its own beat. The trees really were singing, just like Mazy said. It was the same song Lourella used to hum at night, out on the porch. The trees have skin now instead of bark, feathers instead of leaves, and some of them have eyes. The birds that stayed in the swamp are all bigger now, and they've grown teeth and scales. The crocs have all grown big crests on their heads and spines down their backs now. They walk around on their back legs and dance to the music the trees make, and they bow their heads low as we pass by.

We're different too. We've all grown bigger and taller, and we've all got Lourella's yellow eyes, and teeth like you wouldn't believe. The crocs show us respect, because in a way, we're sort of related. Old Ghol, he sort of looked a bit like a croc himself. A lot like, if the truth be told.

Lots of things have changed. We used to go into town for our food occasionally, especially when the hunting wasn't good. Well, we still do, but now we like our food warm, screaming and wailing. Boy, the hunting is sure good in town right now since we tore down the bridge!

When I look up at Sirius at night, I can hear the singing in my head. I know now what's happening. We can't go home, but we don't have to. Our home is growing all around us now. The swamp is gettin' bigger every day, and people outside don't come here anymore. No one comes here from anywhere. They don't have to. The swamp, and everything in it, is coming out to meet them, breathing and hungry. We're coming with it. We are the children of Lourella, daughter of Ghol Dh'ralla Barakyl, lost Prince of the Planet Inh'ralla, third planet of the star you call Canis Major. Sirius, the Dog Star. Me, I like our name better. It means, "Here there be Dragons."

Available now at Wild Child Publishing.com